UNBREAKABLE

UNBREAKABLE

BY KAMI GARCIA

LB

LITTLE, BROWN AND COMPANY

NEW YORK BOSTON

Copyright © 2013 by Kami Garcia, LLC
Excerpt from *Unmarked* copyright © 2014 by Kami Garcia, LLC
Excerpt from *Dangerous Creatures* copyright © 2014 by Kami Garcia, LLC, and Margaret Stohl, Inc.

Little, Brown and Company

Hachette Book Group
237 Park Avenue, New York, NY 10017
Visit our website at lb-teens.com

Little, Brown and Company is a division of Hachette Book Group, Inc.
The Little, Brown name and logo are trademarks of Hachette Book Group, Inc.

The publisher is not responsible for websites (or their content) that are not owned by the publisher.

First Paperback Edition: May 2014
First published in hardcover in October 2013 by Little, Brown and Company

Library of Congress Cataloging-in-Publication Data
Garcia, Kami.
Unbreakable / by Kami Garcia. — First edition.
pages cm
Summary: "Seventeen-year-old Kennedy Waters discovers she is a member of an ancient secret society formed to protect the world from a powerful demon determined to find a way out of his dimension and into ours. She joins the Legion on a mission to find a weapon that can defeat the demon"— Provided by publisher.
ISBN 978-0-316-21017-1 (hc)—ISBN 978-0-316-21018-8 (pb)
[1. Demonology—Fiction. 2. Secret societies—Fiction. 3. Supernatural—Fiction. 4. Love—Fiction.] I. Title.
PZ7.G155627Unb 2013
[Fic]—dc23

2012048435

10 9 8 7 6 5 4 3 2 1

RRD-C

Printed in the United States of America

For Alex, Nick & Stella:
None of the imaginary worlds I create
compare to the real one I share with you.

There are a thousand hacking at the branches of evil to one who is striking at the root.

—Henry David Thoreau, *Walden*

1. SLEEPWALKER

As my bare feet sank into the wet earth, I tried not to think about the dead bodies buried beneath me. I had passed this tiny graveyard a handful of times but never at night, and always outside the boundaries of its peeling iron gates.

I would've given anything to be standing outside them now.

In the moonlight, rows of weathered headstones exposed the neat stretch of lawn for what it truly was—the grassy lid of an enormous coffin.

A branch snapped, and I spun around.

"Elvis?" I searched for a trace of my cat's gray and white ringed tail.

Elvis never ran away, usually content to thread his way

1

between my ankles whenever I opened the door—until tonight. He had taken off so fast that I didn't even have time to grab my shoes, and I had chased him eight blocks until I ended up here.

Muffled voices drifted through the trees, and I froze.

On the other side of the gates, a girl wearing blue and gray Georgetown University sweats passed underneath the pale glow of the lamppost. Her friends caught up with her, laughing and stumbling down the sidewalk. They reached one of the academic buildings and disappeared inside.

It was easy to forget that the cemetery was in the middle of a college campus. As I walked deeper into the uneven rows, the lampposts vanished behind the trees, and the clouds plunged the graveyard in and out of shadow. I ignored the whispers in the back of my mind urging me to go home.

Something moved in my peripheral vision—a flash of white.

I scanned the stones, now completely bathed in black.

Come on, Elvis. Where are you?

Nothing scared me more than the dark. I liked to see what was coming, and darkness was a place where things could hide.

Think about something else.

The memory closed in before I could stop it....

My mother's face hovering above mine as I blinked

myself awake. The panic in her eyes as she pressed a finger over her lips, signaling me to be quiet. The cold floor against my feet as we made our way to her closet, where she pushed aside the dresses.

"Someone's in the house," she whispered, pulling a board away from the wall to reveal a small opening. "Stay here until I come back. Don't make a sound."

I squeezed inside as she worked the board back into place. I had never experienced absolute darkness before. I stared at a spot inches in front of me, where my palm rested on the board. But I couldn't see it.

I closed my eyes against the blackness. There were sounds—the stairs creaking, furniture scraping against the floor, muffled voices—and one thought replaying over and over in my mind.

What if she didn't come back?

Too terrified to see if I could get out from the inside, I kept my hand on the wood. I listened to my ragged breathing, convinced that whoever was in the house could hear it, too.

Eventually, the wood gave beneath my palm and a thin stream of light flooded the space. My mom reached for me, promising the intruders had fled. As she carried me out of her closet, I couldn't hear anything beyond the pounding of my heart, and I couldn't think about anything except the crushing weight of the dark.

I was only five when it happened, but I still remembered

every minute in the crawl space. It made the air around me now feel suffocating. Part of me wanted to go home, with or without my cat.

"Elvis, get out here!"

Something shifted between the chipped headstones in front of me.

"Elvis?"

A silhouette emerged from behind a stone cross.

I jumped, a tiny gasp escaping my lips. "Sorry." My voice wavered. "I'm looking for my cat."

The stranger didn't say a word.

Sounds intensified at a dizzying rate—branches breaking, leaves rustling, my pulse throbbing. I thought about the hundreds of unsolved crime shows I'd watched with my mom that began exactly like this—a girl standing alone somewhere she shouldn't be, staring at the guy who was about to attack her.

I stepped back, thick mud pushing up around my ankles like a hand rooting me to the spot.

Please don't hurt me.

The wind cut through the graveyard, lifting tangles of long hair off the stranger's shoulders and the thin fabric of a white dress from her legs.

Her legs.

Relief washed over me. "Have you seen a gray and white Siamese cat? I'm going to kill him when I find him."

Silence.

Her dress caught the moonlight, and I realized it wasn't a dress at all. She was wearing a nightgown. Who wandered around a cemetery in their nightgown?

Someone crazy.

Or someone sleepwalking.

You aren't supposed to wake a sleepwalker, but I couldn't leave her out here alone at night either.

"Hey? Can you hear me?"

The girl didn't move, gazing at me as if she could see my features in the darkness. An empty feeling unfolded in the pit of my stomach. I wanted to look at something else—anything but her unnerving stare.

My eyes drifted down to the base of the cross.

The girl's feet were as bare as mine, and it looked like they weren't touching the ground.

I blinked hard, unwilling to consider the other possibility. It had to be an effect of the moonlight and the shadows. I glanced at my own feet, caked in mud, and back to hers.

They were pale and spotless.

A flash of white fur darted in front of her and rushed toward me.

Elvis.

I grabbed him before he could get away. He hissed at me, clawing and twisting violently until I dropped him. My heart hammered in my chest as he darted across the grass and squeezed under the gate.

I looked back at the stone cross.

The girl was gone, the ground nothing but a smooth, untouched layer of mud.

Blood from the scratches trailed down my arm as I crossed the graveyard, trying to reason away the girl in the white nightgown.

Silently reminding myself that I didn't believe in ghosts.

2. SCRATCHING THE SURFACE

When I stumbled back onto the well-lit sidewalk, there was no sign of Elvis. A guy with a backpack slung over his shoulder walked by and gave me a strange look when he noticed I was barefoot, and covered in mud up to my ankles. He probably thought I was a pledge.

My hands didn't stop shaking until I hit O Street, where the shadows of the campus ended and the lights of the DC traffic began. Tonight, even the tourists posing for pictures at the top of *The Exorcist* stairs were somehow reassuring.

The cemetery suddenly felt miles away, and I started second-guessing myself.

The girl in the graveyard hadn't been hazy or transparent like the ghosts in movies. She had looked like a regular girl.

Except she was floating.

Wasn't she?

Maybe the moonlight had only made it appear that way. And maybe the girl's feet weren't muddy because the ground where she'd been standing was dry. By the time I reached my block, lined with row houses crushed together like sardines, I convinced myself there were dozens of explanations.

Elvis lounged on our front steps, looking docile and bored. I considered leaving him outside to teach him a lesson, but I loved that stupid cat.

I still remembered the day my mom bought him for me. I came home from school crying because we'd made Father's Day gifts in class, and I was the only kid without a father. Mine had walked away when I was five and never looked back. My mom had wiped my tears and said, "I bet you're also the only kid in your class getting a kitten today."

Elvis had turned one of my worst days into one of my best.

I opened the door, and he darted inside. "You're lucky I let you in."

The house smelled like tomatoes and garlic, and my mom's voice drifted into the hallway. "I've got plans this weekend. Next weekend, too. I'm sorry, but I have to run. I think my daughter just came home. Kennedy?"

"Yeah, Mom."

"Were you at Elle's? I was about to call you."

I stepped into the doorway as she hung up the phone. "Not exactly."

She threw me a quick glance, and the wooden spoon slipped out of her hand and hit the floor, sending a spray of red sauce across the white tile. "What happened?"

"I'm fine. Elvis ran off, and it took forever to catch him."

Mom rushed over and examined the angry claw marks. "Elvis did this? He's never scratched anyone before."

"I guess he freaked out when I grabbed him."

Her gaze dropped to my mud-caked feet. "Where were you?"

I prepared for the standard lecture Mom issued whenever I went out at night: always carry your cell phone, don't walk alone, stay in well-lit areas, and her personal favorite—scream first and ask questions later. Tonight, I had violated them all.

"The old Jesuit cemetery?" My answer sounded more like a question—as in, exactly how upset was she going to be?

Mom stiffened and she drew in a sharp breath. "I'd never go into a graveyard at night," she responded automatically, as though it was something she'd said a thousand times before. Except it wasn't.

"Suddenly you're superstitious?"

She shook her head and looked away. "Of course not.

You don't have to be superstitious to know that secluded places are dangerous at night."

I waited for the lecture.

Instead, she handed me a wet towel. "Wipe off your feet and throw that away. I don't want dirt from a cemetery in my washing machine."

Mom rummaged through the junk drawer until she found a giant Band-Aid that looked like a leftover from my Big Wheel days.

"Who were you talking to on the phone?" I asked, hoping to change the subject.

"Just someone from work."

"Did that *someone* ask you out?"

She frowned, concentrating on my arm. "I'm not interested in dating. One broken heart is enough for me." She bit her lip. "I didn't mean—"

"I know what you meant." My mom had cried herself to sleep for what felt like months after my dad left. I still heard her sometimes.

After she bandaged my arm, I sat on the counter while she finished the marinara sauce. Watching her cook was comforting. It made the cemetery feel even farther away.

She dipped her finger in the pot and tasted the sauce before taking the pan off the stove.

"Mom, you forgot the red pepper flakes."

"Right." She shook her head and forced a laugh.

My mom could've held her own with Julia Child, and

marinara was her signature dish. She was more likely to forget her own name than the secret ingredient. I almost called her on it, but I felt guilty. Maybe she was imagining me in one of those unsolved crime shows.

I hopped down from the counter. "I'm going upstairs to draw."

She stared out the kitchen window, preoccupied. "Mmm…that's a good idea. It will probably make you feel better."

Actually, it wouldn't make me feel anything.

That was the point.

As long as my hand kept moving over the page, my problems disappeared, and I was somewhere or *someone* else for a little while. My drawings were fueled by a world only I could see—a boy carrying his nightmares in a sack as bits and pieces spilled out behind him, or a mouthless man banging away at the keys of a broken typewriter in the dark.

Like the piece I was working on now.

I stood in front of my easel and studied the girl perched on a rooftop, with one foot hanging tentatively over the edge. She stared at the ground below, her face twisted in fear. Delicate blue-black swallow wings stretched out from her dress. The fabric was torn where the wings had ripped through it, growing from her back like the branches of a tree.

I read somewhere that if a swallow builds a nest on your roof, it will bring you good luck. But if it abandons the nest, you'll have nothing but misfortune. Like so many things, the bird could be a blessing or a curse, a fact the girl bearing its wings knew too well.

I fell asleep thinking about her. Wondering what it would be like to have wings if you were too scared to fly.

⊰ • ⊱

I woke up the next morning exhausted. My dreams had been plagued with sleepwalking girls floating in grave-yards. Elvis was curled up on the pillow next to me. I scratched his ears, and he jumped to the floor.

I didn't drag myself out of bed until Elle showed up in the afternoon. She never bothered to call before she came over. The idea that someone might not want to see her would never occur to Elle, a quality I'd envied from the moment we met in seventh grade.

Now she was sprawled on my bed in a sea of candy wrappers, flipping through a magazine while I stood in front of my easel.

"A bunch of people are going to the movies tonight," Elle said. "What are you wearing?"

"I told you I'm staying home."

"Because of that pathetic excuse for a guy who's going to be the starting receiver at community college when we graduate?" Elle asked, in the dangerous tone she reserved for people who made the mistake of hurting someone she cared about.

My stomach dropped. Even after a few weeks, the wound was still fresh.

"Because I didn't get any sleep." I left out the part about the girl in the graveyard. If I started thinking about her, I'd have another night of bad dreams ahead of me.

"You can sleep when you're dead." Elle tossed the magazine on the floor. "And you can't hide in your room every weekend. You're not the one who should be embarrassed."

I dropped a piece of charcoal in the tackle box on the floor and wiped my hands on my overalls. "I think getting dumped because you won't let your boyfriend use you as a cheat sheet rates pretty high on the humiliation scale."

I should've been suspicious when one of the cutest guys in school asked me to help him bring up his history grade so he wouldn't get kicked off the football team. Especially when it was Chris, the quiet guy who had moved from one foster home to another—and someone I'd had a crush on for years. Still, with the highest GPA in History and all my other classes, I was the logical choice.

I just didn't realize that Chris knew why.

The first few years of elementary school, my eidetic memory was a novelty. Back then, I referred to it as photographic, and kids thought it was cool that I could memorize pages of text in only a few seconds. Until we got older, and they realized I didn't have to study to earn higher grades than them. By the time I hit junior high, I had learned how to hide my "unfair advantage," as the other

13

students and their parents called it when they complained to my teachers.

These days, only a handful of my friends knew. At least, that's what I'd thought.

Chris was smarter than everyone assumed. He put in the time when it came to History—and me. Three weeks. That's how long it took before he kissed me. Two more weeks before he called me his girlfriend.

One more week before he asked if I'd let him copy off me during our midterm.

Seeing him at school and pretending I was fine when he cornered me with his half-assed apologies was hard enough. "I didn't mean to hurt you, Kennedy. But school isn't as easy for me as it is for you. A scholarship is my only chance to get out of here. I thought you understood that."

I understood perfectly, which was the reason I didn't want to run into him tonight.

"I'm not going."

Elle sighed. "He won't be there. The team has an away game."

"Fine. But if any of his loser friends are there, I'm leaving."

She headed for the bathroom with her bag and a smug smile. "I'll start getting ready."

I picked at the half inch of black charcoal under my nails. They would require serious scrubbing unless I wanted to look like a mechanic. The giant Band-Aid on my arm

14

already made me look like a burn victim. At least the theater would be dark.

The front door slammed downstairs, and Mom appeared in the hallway a moment later. "Staying home tonight?"

"I wish." I tilted my head toward the bathroom. "Elle's making me go to the movies with her."

"And you're okay with that?" Mom tried to sound casual, but I knew what she was worried about. She had baked brownies and listened to me cry about Chris for weeks.

"He's not going to be there."

She smiled. "Sounds dangerous. You run the risk of having a good time." Then her expression changed, and she was all business. "Do you have cash?"

"Thirty bucks."

"Is your cell charged?"

I pointed to my nightstand, where my phone was plugged in. "Yep."

"Will anyone be drinking?"

"Mom, we're going to a movie, not a party."

"If for some reason there is drinking—"

I cut her off, reciting the rest by heart. "I'll call you and you'll pick me up, no questions asked, no consequences."

She tugged on the strap of my overalls. "Is this what you're wearing? It's a good look."

"Grunge is coming back. I'm ahead of the curve."

Mom walked over to the easel. She put her arm around

me, leaning her head against mine. "You're so talented, and I can barely draw a straight line. You certainly didn't get it from me."

We ignored the other possible source.

She looked at the black dust coating my hands. "Earth-shattering talent aside, maybe you should take a shower."

"I agree." Elle emerged from the bathroom, ready enough for both of us in tight jeans and a tank top strategically falling off one shoulder. Whoever she planned to flirt with tonight would definitely notice her, along with all the other guys in the theater. Even in a tangled ponytail and barely any makeup, Elle was hard to miss.

Another difference between us.

I wandered into the bathroom, my expectations for myself considerably lower. Getting rid of the charcoal under my nails would be a win.

Mom and Elle were whispering when I came back out.

"What's the big secret?"

"Nothing." Mom raised a shopping bag in the air, dangling it by the handle. "I just picked up something for you. I thought you might need them. Evidence of my psychic powers."

I recognized the logo printed on the side. "Are those what I think they are?"

She shrugged. "I don't know...."

I pulled out the box and tossed the lid on the floor.

Resting in the folds of tissue paper was a pair of black boots with leather straps that buckled up the sides. I'd seen them a few weeks ago when we were shopping. They were perfect—different, but not too different.

"I thought they'd look great with your uniform," she said, referring to the black jeans and faded T-shirts I wore every day.

"They'll look amazing with anything." I pulled on the boots and checked myself out in the mirror.

Elle nodded her approval. "Definitely cool."

"They'll probably look better without the bathrobe." Mom waved a black tube in the air. "And maybe with a little mascara?"

I hated mascara. It was like fingerprints at the scene of a crime. If you cried, it was impossible to get rid of the black smudges under your eyes, which was almost as embarrassing as crying in front of everyone in the first place.

"It's only a movie, and that stuff gets all over my face whenever I put it on." Or hours later, something I learned the hard way.

"There's a trick." Mom stood in front of me, brandishing the wand. "Look up."

I gave in, hoping it might make me look more like Elle and less like the girl-next-door.

Elle leaned over my mom's shoulder, checking out her technique as she applied a sticky coat. "I would kill for those eyelashes, and you don't even appreciate them."

Mom stepped back and admired her work, then glanced at Elle. "What do you think?"

"Gorgeous." Elle flopped down on the bed dramatically. "Mrs. Waters, you are the coolest."

"Be home by midnight or I'll seem a lot less cool," she said on her way out.

Elvis peeked around the corner.

I walked over to pick him up. He froze for a moment, his eyes fixed on me. Then he tore back down the hall.

"What's the deal with the King?" Elle asked, using her favorite nickname for Elvis.

"He's been acting weird." I didn't want to elaborate.

I wanted to forget about the graveyard and the girl in the white nightgown. But I couldn't shake the image of her feet hovering above the ground—or the feeling that there was a reason I couldn't stop thinking about her.

3. BLACKOUT

The house was dark when Elle dropped me off five minutes before curfew, which was strange because Mom always waited up. She liked to hang out in the kitchen while I raided the fridge and gave her a slightly edited play-by-play of the night. After my self-imposed exile, she'd be amused when I reported that nothing had changed.

Elle had dragged me around the lobby with her while she flirted with guys she would never go out with, and I got stuck making awkward small talk with their friends. At least it was over and no one had asked about Chris.

I unlocked the door.

She hadn't even left a light on for me.

"Mom?"

Maybe she fell asleep.

I flipped the switch at the base of the stairs. Nothing. The power was probably out.

Great.

The house was pitch-black. A rush of dizziness swept over me as the fear started to build.

My hand curled around the banister, and I focused on the top of the stairs trying to convince myself it wasn't that dark.

I crept up the steps. "Mom?"

When I reached the second-floor landing, a rush of cold air knocked the breath out of my lungs. The temperature inside must have dropped at least twenty degrees since I left for the movies. Did we leave a window open?

"Mom!"

The lights flickered, casting long shadows down the narrow hallway. I stumbled toward her room, my panic increasing with every step. The memory of the tiny crawl space in the back of her closet fought to break free.

Don't think about it.

I edged closer.

This end of the hall was even colder, and my breath came out in white puffs. Her door was open, a pale yellow light blinking inside.

The stench of stale cigarette smoke hit me, and a rising sense of dread clawed at my insides.

Someone's in the house.

I stepped through the doorway, and the wrongness of the scene closed in on me.

My mom lay on the bed, motionless.

Elvis crouched on her chest.

The lamp in the corner flashed on and off like a child was toying with the switch.

The cat made a low guttural sound that cut through the silence, and I shuddered. If an animal could scream, that was what it would sound like.

"Mom?"

Elvis' head whipped around in my direction.

I ran to the bed and he leapt to the floor.

My mother's head was tilted to the side, dark hair spilling across her face, as the room pitched in and out of darkness. I realized how still she was—the fact that her chest wasn't rising and falling. I pressed my fingers against her throat.

Nothing.

I shook her roughly. "Mom, wake up!"

Tears streamed down my face, and I slid my hand under her cheek. The light stopped flashing, bathing the room in a faint glow.

"Mom!" I grabbed her shoulders and yanked her

upright. Her head swung forward and fell against her chest. I scrambled backward, and her body dropped down onto the mattress, bouncing against it unnaturally.

I slid to the floor, choking on my tears.

My mother's head lay against the bed at an awkward angle, her face turned toward me.

Her eyes were as empty as a doll's.

FOUR WEEKS LATER

4. GRAVE JUMPING

My bedroom still looked like my bedroom, the bookshelves crammed with sketch pads and tins filled with broken pencils and bits of charcoal. The bed was still positioned in the center like an island, so I could lie on my back and stare at the posters and drawings taped to my walls. Chris Berens' *Lady Day* still hung on the back of my door—a beautiful girl imprisoned in a glass dome floating across the sky. I had spent more than a few nights inventing stories about the girl trapped inside. In the end, she always found a way out.

Now I wasn't so sure.

I had two days to take this place apart and box up everything that mattered to me. The things that made this room mine—the things that defined me. I'd tried a hundred times over the last month, but I couldn't bring myself to do it. So I enlisted the only person left who loved this place almost as much as I did.

"Earth to Kennedy? Did you hear anything I said?" Elle held up one of my sketchbooks. "Do you want these in the box with art stuff or in the one with books?"

I shrugged. "Whatever you think."

I stood in front of the mirror, pulling out the faded photos tucked around the edge: a blurry close-up of Elvis swatting at the lens as a kitten. My mom wearing cutoffs at about my age, washing a black Camaro and waving a soapy hand at the camera, the silver ID bracelet she never took off still dangling from her wrist.

A nurse at the hospital had handed me a clear plastic bag with that bracelet inside the night my mom was pronounced dead. She'd found me in the waiting room, sitting in the same yellow chair where the doctor had spoken the two words that shattered my life: *heart failure*.

Now the bracelet was fastened around my wrist, and the plastic bag with my mom's name printed at the top was tucked inside my oldest sketchbook.

Elle reached for a picture of the two of us with our tongues sticking out, mouths stained cotton candy blue. "I can't believe you're really leaving."

"It's not like I have a choice. Boarding school is better than living with my aunt." My mom and her sister hardly spoke, and the few times I did see them in the same room, they had been at each other's throats. My aunt was just another stranger, like my father. I didn't want to live with a woman I barely knew and listen to her promise me that everything would be okay.

I wanted to let the pain fill me up and coat my insides with the armor I needed to make it through this. I imagined the dome from *Lady Day* lowering itself over me.

But instead of glass, mine was made of steel.

Unbreakable.

I didn't explain any of that to my aunt when I refused to move to Boston to live with her, or when she had spread out a stack of glossy boarding school brochures in front of me a few days later. I had flipped through the pictures of ivy-covered buildings that all looked frighteningly similar: Pennsylvania, Rhode Island, Connecticut. In the end, I picked upstate New York, the coldest place—and the farthest from home.

My aunt had started making arrangements immediately, as if she wanted to go back to her life as badly as I wanted to get her out of mine. I had forced a wave when her cab finally pulled away from the curb yesterday, after I persuaded her to let me stay at Elle's until I left for New York.

As I pulled the picture of Elvis off the mirror, another photo fluttered to the floor—my dad standing in front of a gray weather-beaten house with me grinning from his shoulders. I looked so happy, like nothing could wipe that smile off my face. It reminded me of a darker day, when I learned that a smile can break as easily as a heart.

I woke up early and tiptoed downstairs to watch cartoons with the volume muted, the way I usually did when my parents slept late on weekends. I was pouring chocolate milk into my cereal when I heard the hinges of the front door groan. I rushed to the window.

My dad had his back to me, a duffel bag in one hand and his car keys in the other.

Was he going on a trip?

He opened the driver's-side door and bent down to climb in. That's when he saw me and froze. I waved, and he raised his hand as if he was going to wave back. But he never did. Instead, he closed the car door and drove away.

I found the ripped sheet of paper on the table in the hall a few minutes later. Sloppy handwriting stretched across the page like a scar.

Elizabeth

You're the first woman I ever loved, and I know you'll be the last. But I can't stay. All I ever wanted for us—and for Kennedy—was a normal life. I think we both know that's impossible.

Alex

I couldn't read the words back then, but my brain took a mental snapshot, preserving the curve of every letter.

Years later, I realized what it said and the reason my father left. It was the note my mom had cried over night after night, and the one she'd never discuss.

What could she say? Your dad left because he wanted a normal daughter? She would never have admitted something that cruel to me, even if it were true.

Swallowing hard, I forced the note out of my mind. I saw it often enough already.

I grabbed a roll of packing tape as Elvis darted into the room. He jumped up on the edge of the box in front of me. When I reached out to pet him, he sprang to the floor and disappeared down the hall again.

Elle rolled her eyes. "I'm glad I agreed to take your psychotic cat while you're away at school."

A knot formed at the base of my throat. Leaving Elvis behind felt like losing another part of my mom.

I pushed the pain down deeper. "You know he's not usually like this. It's hard for animals to adjust when someone they love"—I still couldn't say it—"when they lose someone."

She was quiet for a moment before slipping back into her easy banter. "How much longer do you think this will take? I want to order pizza so it'll be there when we get to my house."

I surveyed the half-packed boxes and piles of clothes scattered around my room. In two days, a driver was coming to pick up the pieces of my life and take them to a school I had only seen in a brochure. "Is it weird if I want to stay here tonight?"

Elle raised an eyebrow. "That would be a yes."

I stared at my walls, the plaster underneath exposed where I had peeled off bits of tape. "I just want it to be my room a little longer, you know?"

"I get it. But my mom will never go for it."

I shot her a pathetic look.

She sighed. "I'll call her and tell her we're staying at Jen's."

"I kind of wanted to stay by myself."

Elle's eyes widened. "You can't be serious."

I didn't know how to explain it, but I wasn't ready to leave. Part of my mom would always be in this house, at least my memories of her. Breaking up chocolate bars in the kitchen to make her extreme brownies. Watching her paint my bedroom walls violet to match my favorite stuffed animal. Those were things that I couldn't pack in boxes.

"My aunt is selling the house. It'll probably be the last time I get to sleep in my room."

Elle shook her head, but I knew she was going to give in. "I'll stay at Jen's and tell my mom you're with me." She walked over to my dresser and picked up the photo of the two of us with our blue tongues, the edges bending beneath the pressure of her fingers. "Don't forget this one."

"You keep it." My voice cracked.

Her eyes welled, and she threw her arms around me. "I'm gonna miss you so much."

"We still have two more days." Two days seemed like forever. I would've killed for two more *hours* with my mom.

After Elle left, I peeled the yellowed tape off the edges of Berens' *The Great Escape*. I tossed the poster in the trash, wishing I could escape from the cardboard boxes and the bare walls and a life that didn't feel anything like the one I remembered.

⊰ • ⊱

I drifted in and out of sleep, fragments of dreams cutting through my consciousness. My mom's body lying motionless on the bed. Her empty eyes staring at me. A bitter cold wrapping itself around me like a wet blanket. The sensation of something bearing down on my chest.

I struggled to sit up, but the weight was too heavy.

It felt like someone was holding a pillow over my face. I reached out blindly, trying to push it away. But there was no pillow. Just the air I couldn't breathe and the weight I couldn't move.

Blinking hard, I searched for something familiar to pull me out of the dream. There was nothing except a blurry silhouette looming above me.

No. On top of me.

Two eyes glittered in the darkness.

A strangled scream caught in my throat as the pressure bearing down on my chest intensified, and the room began to fade....

Sounds brought me back—a crash, banging on the stairs, voices. The hall lights flickered, and I finally saw what was hiding behind those luminous eyes.

Elvis—crouched on my chest, mouth open and eyes locked on mine.

I inhaled sharply, but there was still no air. Elvis' ears flattened against his head, and his jaw pulled back like a snake about to strike.

The bedroom door banged against the wall, and someone shouted, "Take the shot!"

Elvis whipped around toward the voice, and a rush of air burned through my lungs. A guy stood in the doorway with something black in his hand.

Who—

He raised his arm.

Was that a gun?

A shot rang out, and the weight lifted. I sat up, gasping and choking on the air my body so desperately needed. A sticky mist rained down over everything, stinging my eyes, and I squeezed them shut.

When I opened them again, I was too stunned to make a sound.

At the foot of my bed, a girl floated in the air

above Elvis' body. Pale and gaunt, her face marred with bruises and cuts, her blond hair hanging in tangled curls.

Bare feet dangled beneath her white nightgown.

It was the girl from the graveyard. Her bloodshot eyes found mine, frozen in a moment of pure terror. The girl's neck was marked with two purple bruises, perfect imprints of the hands that must have killed her.

A second shot hit the strangled girl's body, and she exploded. Millions of tiny particles fluttered in the air like dust before vanishing completely.

Hands touched my shoulders. "Are you okay?"

Our faces were only inches apart—a guy about my age, wearing a black nylon flight jacket.

I scrambled backward. "Who are you?"

"My name is Lukas Lockhart, and that's my brother, Jared." He looked over at a guy standing by the door in a green army jacket with the name LOCKHART on a patch sewn above the pocket. A pale scar cut across the skin above his eyebrow.

They were both tall and broad-shouldered, with the same messy brown hair and blue eyes.

Identical twins.

The one in the army jacket walked over to Elvis' body, a gun wrapped in silver duct tape still in his hand.

The gun that killed my cat.

My stomach lurched, and I bolted off the bed.

"Wait!" one of them shouted, his footsteps practically on top of mine.

The staircase at the end of the hall was too far and he was too close. I'd never make it. But the bathroom was only a few feet away.

I slammed the door behind me and locked it.

The knob rattled a second later. "It's Lukas. We just want to help."

I couldn't think straight. Something that looked like a dead girl had just exploded in my bedroom, and now I was alone in the house with two guys I didn't know. They had definitely saved my life....

But one of them has a gun.

"You killed my cat."

"It's not dead. It took off out the window." His voice sounded soothing and gentle, which only made me more anxious. "Those were liquid-salt rounds."

I gasped, remembering the sticky mist in my bedroom. "So he's okay?"

"Your cat's probably freaked out," he said. "But he was alive the last time I saw him."

Tears of relief ran down my cheeks. "What was that thing inside him?"

Thinking about the girl's tormented expression and the dark bruises around her neck made my skin crawl.

Something horrible must have happened to her—whatever she was.

There was a long pause, followed by whispering on the other side of the door.

"She was a vengeance spirit," Lukas said. "They manifest when a person suffers a violent or traumatic death."

I thought about the night in the cemetery and the walk home, when I'd tried to convince myself that I hadn't seen a girl floating in the graveyard. "A spirit? You mean, like a ghost?"

"Yeah. A really pissed off one." Another voice passed through the door. It was harder, like the kindness had been hammered out of it. Lukas' brother—what was his name? Jared.

"I think I've seen it before—the ghost."

"When?" Jared sounded worried.

"A month ago, in the cemetery a few blocks from here." More whispering. "What did it want with me?"

They were silent for a moment before Lukas answered, "She was using the cat to steal your breath. Vengeance spirits are angry or confused about their deaths, so they attack the living."

The image of Elvis crouched on my mom's chest flashed through my mind, and a wave of nausea racked my body. She didn't die of a heart attack.

I barely made it to the toilet before my stomach lurched.

Someone knocked softly. "You okay?"

My mom was dead, and according to two strangers, an angry spirit had killed her—the same one that had just tried to kill me.

"How did the spirit get inside my cat?" It sounded ridiculous. But I could still feel the unbearable pressure on my chest.

"Most likely by grave jumping. An animal walks·over a fresh grave and the spirit hitches a ride." It was Jared, the one with the gun.

I pictured Elvis walking over the girl's grave and her ghostly hand shooting up from the ground and grabbing his furry leg. They couldn't be serious. "Sounds like a crazy superstition."

"That superstition almost killed you," Jared said.

I pressed the heels of my hands against my eyes. "Well, I'm fine now. You can go."

"It's not safe, Kennedy. You should come with us."

Regardless of what happened in my room, two guys had broken into my house and they were standing in the hallway, armed. I glanced at the window. The last streaks of darkness were fading from the sky, but the sidewalks remained empty.

"I have my cell," I bluffed. "Leave, or I'm calling the police."

"Will you—"

"I'm dialing."

36

Eventually, I heard the stairs creak.

I didn't come out until the front door slammed. I leaned against the wall, staring at my bedroom door, as a question fought its way from the back of my mind.

How did they know my name?

5. DEAD ENDS

The girl's tortured expression and the handprints around her neck kept coming back to me, no matter how loud I blasted Velvet Revolver. Even worse, when it wasn't her face, it was my mother's empty stare.

My mom was dead because of that girl—or something like her.

The thought had sent me tearing out of the house as soon as the guys left. I had spent hours looking for Elvis, but there was no sign of him. I doubted he would come back to the house. At least he was alive.

Now I was driving around aimlessly on a Saturday morning with nowhere to go.

I almost called Elle, but what could I say? Two guys broke into my house and shot a ghost that tried to kill me?

I'm too scared to go home and—oh, did I mention that I've lost all touch with reality?

Elle checked our horoscopes every morning, and she'd stayed inside for two days after a palm reader told her that her "future was uncertain," but a ghost possessing my cat was pushing it. Convincing her that I didn't need therapy for post-traumatic stress disorder after my mom died had been hard enough.

The light turned red, and I closed my eyes for a second. With the adrenaline rush over, my head pounded. I took a deep breath and tried to relax, when a horn blared behind me.

My eyes flew open to a green light.

I was too exhausted to keep driving around like this.

I pulled into the nearest driveway. At nine thirty in the morning, the lot at the public library was practically empty. Maybe I could sleep for a little while. I locked the doors, unable to shake the feeling that someone, or something, was following me.

I tried to piece together the scene in my bedroom, but the ghost and the gun and the voices were all tangled up in my mind like a pile of broken necklaces. I only remembered snippets of the conversation with Jared and Lukas.

Something about angry spirits? No—vengeance spirits. That's what they called them.

Two girls walked past my window carrying armloads of grad school prep books. I climbed out of the car and followed them into the library. I needed answers, and this was a good place to start.

I found an empty computer station and typed *vengeance spirits* into the search field. I scrolled through pages of articles, reading the ones that seemed the most legitimate and the least crazy. The consensus among paranormal investigators was pretty consistent when it came to the definition—malevolent spirits who haunt or seek to harm the living; usually victims of murder, violence, or suicide; spirits that may, or may not, know they're dead.

Lukas and Jared Lockhart weren't the only ones who believed in this stuff.

There were hundreds of sites dedicated to paranormal activity. I had actually witnessed more in my room than most so-called investigators had in a lifetime, and it still didn't seem possible.

Researching grave jumping was harder. It was classified under myths, folklore, or urban legends, depending on the website. Some articles claimed that if you walked over a fresh grave, the spirit could leap out and turn you into a vampire. Others validated Jared's version in which the spirit jumped inside a person or an animal. It sounded ridiculous, but I still wasn't about to step on a grave anytime soon.

The Internet wasn't going to answer all my questions. I needed to figure out who Lukas and Jared Lockhart were, and what they were doing in my neighborhood at five o'clock in the morning, carrying a gun loaded with salt.

First, I had to find them.

A general search for their names led to information on a dead poet, a German family crest, and the drummer from a punk band. Maybe I was spelling them wrong. I should've asked if they could write their names down before I kicked them out of my house.

"Can I help you find something?" A young and eager-looking librarian stood behind me.

"Um, is there a way to see if someone attends one of the local high schools?"

"Not online. But you can try the reference room."

"What's in there?"

The librarian headed toward the stacks. "Yearbooks."

She led me to the back of the library and unlocked the door to the reference room, where dusty public school yearbooks were lined up on an even dustier shelf. "Let me know if I can help you with anything else."

"Thanks."

I ran my finger along the rows of leather volumes with tacky silver and gold lettering, estimating how long it would take to flip through them all. Lukas and Jared looked about my age or a little older, so I started with ones from last year.

My cell rang and Elle's name popped up on the screen.

I tried to sound grouchy and half asleep, the way I usually did when she called this early. "Hey."

"I'm starving. Wanna get breakfast?" Hearing her voice made the last six hours seem surreal.

"I still have a ton of packing." I fought the urge to tell her everything. Even if I knew she'd believe me—which I didn't—this definitely warranted a face-to-face conversation. "Let's meet up when I'm done."

Then maybe I'll tell you about the ghost that tried to kill me.

"I have rehearsal until nine tonight, remember? I can't blow it off again or my understudy will totally try to steal my part." Elle had scored a lead role in the school musical and developed an unhealthy paranoia when it came to her understudy. "You can come hang out and witness the suckage firsthand."

"Tempting, but I'll pass. See you at your house at nine thirty."

Elle hesitated. "You sound weird. Is everything okay?"

Everything is completely screwed up and confusing and in no way okay.

I took a deep breath. "Yeah, I'm fine."

"Don't be late. It's your last night." She hung up before I had time to say good-bye.

Reaching for a dingy white yearbook at the top of the stack, I flipped through the pages of football games and homecoming candids until I hit class photos.

Identical twins wouldn't be hard to spot.

If I figured out where Jared and Lukas went to school,

maybe I could track down an e-mail address or a phone number. It was a long shot. But I needed to do something—to take control of a situation that felt completely out of control.

By the time I closed the last creased leather cover, it was getting dark outside, and I didn't know any more about Lukas and Jared Lockhart than when I started.

I should've been at home packing. A driver was taking me to the airport in the morning—a fact that I'd made peace with before I found out what really happened to my mother.

⇥ • ⇤

I pulled into the only space on the street in front of my house, letting the engine idle as I listened to the last few verses of the Cure's "Inbetween Days." My world felt that way. Trapped in between the days before it fell apart and the ones I lived in now.

I climbed out of the car, and my throat went dry.

Even with its Kelly green door and trimmed boxwoods lining the walkway, when I looked at my house, all I could see was the dead girl in my bedroom.

Were there other spirits in the house? Could they hurt me if I was awake?

I turned away, trying to summon the courage to go back inside.

A black van was parked across the street, facing the opposite direction. It looked like the ones serial killers use to abduct their victims. The driver noticed me staring and jerked away from the window.

Walking up to a stranger's car felt crazy, but there were plenty of university students on the sidewalks. Even a psycho wouldn't kidnap me in front of witnesses. My eyes darted to the license plate for a second just in case: AL-0381.

My knees turned to rubber as I knocked on the driver's-side window.

It rolled down slowly.

Jared Lockhart stared back at me, still wearing his green army jacket.

I must have been in serious shock last night because I didn't remember him being this gorgeous. Intense blue eyes and full lips, balanced by a roughness that came from a fight or two, kept him from looking like your average pretty boy.

"How long have you been out here?" I couldn't believe I'd spent the whole day trying to find him and his brother, and they were sitting in front of my house.

Jared shrugged sheepishly. "Awhile."

Lukas leaned forward in the passenger seat, rolling a silver coin over his fingers. "Glad you're happier to see us this time."

"I'm sorry about last night. But I've never seen any-thing like that before."

Lukas threw me a crooked smile. "Apology accepted.

I'm just glad we got there when we did." He seemed sincere, and something inside me relaxed.

"You guys showed up out of nowhere," I said. "How did you know I needed help?"

Jared's eyes darted from me to his brother.

"We heard you screaming." Lukas didn't miss a beat. "Your window was open, remember?"

How could I forget—struggling to breathe, the pressure on my chest, almost suffocating. Screaming was the only part I didn't remember. They weren't telling me everything. I just didn't know why.

"Do you guys carry around a gun full of salt and shoot ghosts every night?"

Jared shifted uncomfortably in his seat. "It's kind of a hobby."

A hobby? He made it sound like they were playing video games, and I was scared to walk into my own house.

"But I'm safe now? I mean, there's nothing else in my house, right?"

Jared frowned, his scar disappearing between the worry lines in his forehead. "Those are two different questions."

Lukas' smile faded. "Jared, we have to tell her. She's in danger."

My skin went cold.

What was inside? The ghosts of other dead girls?

"I thought you got rid of the spirit."

"We did." Jared stared into the growing darkness. "But he'll send others."

"Who?" My voice wavered.

Lukas stopped rolling the coin and looked at me. "The demon that's trying to kill you."

6. SINISTER LULLABY

"Let me get this straight. A demon is sending these vengeance spirits to kill people?"

It was hard to believe we were having this conversation at the table where I ate my cereal every morning. It wasn't that I'd never considered the possibility of ghosts, especially after my mom died. I wanted to imagine her out there somewhere in a better place. But a vengeance spirit possessing my cat and murdering my mom was on a completely different level. And now we were talking demons.

Lukas watched me from across the table, measuring my reactions. "The demon isn't sending them after just anyone. He wants them to kill specific people. And you're one of them."

It didn't make any sense. "Why me?"

47

Jared had been pacing the room like a caged animal since we came inside. He stopped and turned to his brother, a silent question passing between them. Lukas nodded, and Jared took something out of his pocket. A tattered sheet of yellowed parchment, the creases so deep it practically fell apart when he unfolded it.

Jared slid the paper across the table. "Have you ever seen this?"

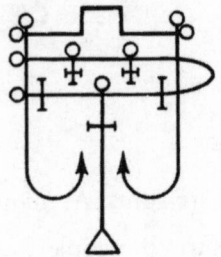

A hand-drawn symbol filled the center of the page. It reminded me of a music stand with two lines curving upward, each capped with a triangle like the devil's tail. "No."

"Are you sure?" Jared's eyes drilled into me.

Of course I was. A basic image composed of three continuous lines wasn't a stretch with a memory like mine. Not that I was admitting that to them.

I studied the symbol for their benefit. "I'd remember something like that. Are you going to tell me what it is?"

"It's a seal." Lukas took the silver coin he'd been toying with earlier out of his pocket. It looked like a quarter, but the image was different. His fingers rose and fell in a steady rhythm as the coin rolled over them and back again. "Every demon has a unique seal, like a signature. It's used to summon and command the demon. This one belongs to Andras."

Now the demon has a name?

Jared reached for the page, and his hand grazed mine. He yanked it away like he was allergic to human contact, and shoved his hands in his pockets.

"Ever heard of the Illuminati?" Lukas asked.

The name was familiar. They were one of those conspiracy groups featured on the History Channel all the time. "Like the Knights Templar?"

"They were both secret societies, but the Templars fought *for* the Catholic Church, and the Illuminati wanted to destroy it."

I paused before asking the next question, testing out the words in my mind. There was no way to make them sound right. "What do they have to do with the demon?"

The one I don't know if I believe in? The one that's trying to kill me?

"I'll give you the short version, but it won't make sense unless I start at the beginning."

I stayed quiet, encouraging Lukas to continue.

"In 1776, five guys in Bavaria formed the Illuminati. They wanted to take down the governments and churches so they could create some kind of new world order. They targeted the Catholic Church and decided that killing the pope would be a good place to start."

"So they were insane?"

"Pretty much." Lukas leaned forward, resting his arms on the table. "The church formed a secret society of its own—the Legion of the Black Dove. Five excommunicated priests with orders to destroy the Illuminati."

I wondered if Lukas had seen too many of those documentaries. "Why were they excommunicated?"

"Different reasons." He gave me an awkward half-smile. "Let's just say none of them played by the rules."

"Five people doesn't sound like much of a legion."

Jared stopped pacing. "It's a reference from the Bible. Jesus met a man who was possessed, and he commanded the demon to tell him its name. The demon said, 'My name is Legion: for we are many.'" Jared's deep voice grew quieter. "The ex-priests called themselves the Legion to remind them of what they were fighting. And of what they had to become in order to win."

I didn't know where they were going with this.

"But there was a problem," Lukas said. "Since no one knew the identities of the Illuminati members, they were impossible to stop. So the Legion turned to a grimoire."

"A what?"

He watched me for a moment before answering. "Grimoires are texts that provide instructions for communicating with angels...or summoning and commanding demons. The Legion used one to call Andras."

Angels? Summoning demons?

I stared back at him, speechless.

Lukas walked over to the empty cabinets and rummaged around, unearthing a forgotten coffee mug. He filled it with water from the faucet and handed it to me. "I know all this might sound unbelievable—"

"You think it *might* sound unbelievable?" I stood up and leaned against the refrigerator behind me, the bite of cold metal spreading up my back. "Which part? The fact that demons exist or that one's trying to kill me?"

"When you say it like that, it does sound kind of stupid," Lukas said. "But it's still true."

Before I had a chance to respond, the radio on the counter switched on. The dial turned and the needle moved across the stations, snippets of voices and songs distorting into a single progression.

"There's a storm warning—"

"—electrical storms tearing across the sky—"

"—three deaths reported—"

"—killed tragically—"

"—looking for salvation—"

Finally, it stopped on an Alice in Chains track, a single line repeating slowly over the crackle of static.

"Ain't found a way to kill me yet—"

The cord dangled from the counter.

Unplugged.

"Ain't found a way to kill me yet—"

Lukas reached out his hand, urging me toward him. "Kennedy—"

The wooden cabinets began to rattle, and the faucet turned itself on full blast. Steam rose from the sink. Jared shouted something, but I couldn't hear anything except the ominous message repeating over and over.

"Ain't found a way to kill me yet—"

Something metallic glinted in my peripheral vision. A knife block sat next to the stove, directly across from the kitchen doorway. I hadn't bothered to pack it because it weighed a ton.

The black handles of the knives were still secure in their slots. Except for one.

A steak knife hovered above the counter. It turned slowly until the blade faced Lukas. For a moment, it didn't move.

"Ain't found a way to kill me yet—"

The knife tore through the air.

"Lukas!" I screamed.

He pivoted as the blade hit the doorframe, catching the edge of his jacket.

Another knife slid out, the serrated edge skimming the wood as it pulled free.

Jared ran toward me. "Move!"

"Ain't found a way to kill me yet—"

The garbage disposal whirred to life, spraying hot water

from the sink all over the room. I shielded my face with one arm and reached out for Jared blindly with the other.

The second knife landed next to me, with the clipped sound of metal against metal as it hit the fridge.

Someone grabbed me around the waist and hauled me out of the kitchen. I wiped my eyes, hot water trailing down my neck. I caught a glimpse of his army jacket and realized it was Jared. He was soaked, water running down his face, a single-minded focus propelling him forward. Jared's hand locked on my hip, his fingers pressed against me, as if nothing could break that hold.

Lukas was at the front door, yanking on the handle. "It won't open."

I glanced through the kitchen doorway. The remaining ten knives drew themselves from the block one by one and lined up in the air.

There was no way we could dodge that many.

"Get out of the way." Jared released me and pushed his brother aside. He pulled the duct tape-covered gun out of his jacket and fired three shots at the base of the door. Steam poured from holes where the salt rounds gouged the wood.

He looked at Lukas, who was already backing up. "We have to break it down."

Jared and Lukas charged the door. Their shoulders slammed into it simultaneously, but the hinges only groaned. They backed up again.

This time, I threw my body against the door alongside theirs. I heard the wood crack and felt myself falling....

I skidded across the front walk, my hands burning as they scraped the pavement. I waited for the world around me to stop swaying before I turned back to my house.

Lights flashed on and off inside like an insidious form of Morse code.

"Kennedy." Fear and panic warred in Jared's eyes. He grabbed my hand and pulled me up. "We have to get to the van."

Lukas was already halfway there.

I couldn't take my eyes off the house as I ran. It was alive—breathing, consuming, destroying. The kitchen windows exploded, spraying glass all over the sidewalk.

Jared yanked the van door open and shoved me across the bench seat toward Lukas. The air in front of the house started to move like the tide pulling back from the shore—sucking broken glass, splintered wood, and potted plants up the sidewalk and into its jaws, as the house took one long, devastating breath.

"Look what it's doing." Lukas' eyes widened.

The supernatural force pulling everything inside suddenly stopped. The air in the front hall started to churn like a tiny cyclone, our welcome mat and one of my sneakers caught in the brown whirlwind.

Inside, the lights flickered faster and faster.

Lukas glanced from Jared to the house. "Hurry up."

Jared fumbled to get the keys in the ignition.

"What's happening?"

A surge of air burst from the hallway like a bomb exploding, tearing what was left of the front door right off its hinges and expelling everything the house had sucked in.

The van pulled away from the curb. I stared out the back window watching as other doors along my street opened, my house growing smaller and smaller.

Was I really leaving with them?

It wasn't a question anymore.

I had made my decision when I became more than just a girl with a dead mother—somewhere between the girl in the white nightgown, the knives flying, and the cyclone in the hallway. I was a girl whose mother was taken from her by something supernatural.

And something evil.

7. THE LEGION

That was the nastiest poltergeist I've ever seen." Lukas looked out the window one last time like he hoped to catch another glimpse.

"It's the only one you've ever seen." Jared kept his eyes on the road, his expression tense.

"Whatever. That was some serious energy."

They were talking about it like a hurricane or a tornado, but it wasn't some uncontrollable natural disaster. It was completely *unnatural*, controlled in a way I didn't understand. And judging from Jared's comment, they weren't experts either.

I wrapped my arms around myself.

"Are you cold?" Lukas started to take off his jacket.

"I'm fine," I said.

We both knew I was lying. It was December, and I was wearing my standard uniform, skinny black jeans and a thin gray T-shirt. I would've killed for a coat, but I didn't want them to see how far from fine I really was. Lukas didn't push.

Maybe he sensed how lost I felt. Lukas and Jared had at least some of the answers, and I didn't even know the questions. But after the last few hours, I was too exhausted to try to figure them out.

I leaned heavily on one arm, and my hand slid across the seat and bumped into Jared's. Our fingertips touched for a second. He glanced down at them before I pulled away, folding my hands awkwardly in my lap.

"So what happened back there?" I asked.

"A poltergeist," Lukas said.

"Like the movie?"

"Did it feel like a movie?" A reassuring smile played across Lukas' lips. Jared never seemed to smile. Aside from their clothes and Jared's scar, it was one of the few ways I could tell them apart.

"Not one I'd want to see again." I tried to relax, but it was impossible with my body wedged between them.

"That movie was actually pretty accurate. Poltergeists are paranormal entities that feed off energy—electrical, mechanical, even human—and use it to move objects and cause some serious damage. No one knows exactly what they are, but they're not spirits." It sounded like Lukas was repeating something he read on one of those paranormal websites.

"I still don't understand what one was doing in my house."

They both looked away.

"You guys showed up in my bedroom out of nowhere, shot my cat with a gun that looked like something from a video game, and told me that a demon's trying to kill me. Want to explain how you could possibly know that?"

Jared looked over at me. "Because our family has been fighting his army for over two hundred years."

"What are you talking about?"

"Andras can influence vengeance spirits, and he uses them to do what he can't—hurt and kill the living," Lukas said. "The Legion vowed to protect the world from those attacks."

"You mean like those ghost hunters on TV?"

Jared frowned. "More like exorcists."

"I thought exorcists help people who are possessed by demons…or whatever." I wasn't ready to start talking about the devil. I sounded insane enough already.

"Anything can be possessed—places, animals, even objects," Jared explained. "And demons don't have the market cornered. Spirits possess things all the time, like your cat."

I didn't want to think about it. I hoped that Elvis was curled up in front of the fireplace in one of my neighbors' houses.

Lukas squeezed my shoulder gently. "Exorcists are like supernatural exterminators. If something is hanging around that isn't supposed to be there, they get rid of it. For the Legion, that's a full-time job."

How could the world they were describing possibly exist within the one I had lived in my whole life?

Angels and demons? Ghosts that can possess whatever they want, and a secret society of exorcists...

"Are you telling me that someone in your family was part of the Legion?"

"The responsibility has been passed down, each member choosing a blood descendant to assume the duty at the time of their death. It's been that way since the night our ancestors accidentally set Andras free."

For a moment I didn't respond. I watched them—Jared scowling at the road, Lukas with his boots on the dashboard. Neither of them looked delusional, and they definitely knew something about getting rid of vengeful spirits. But the rest of it sounded like an old family legend—a story that someone had misrepresented as history. Were their parents crazy? Conspiracy theorists who had passed on their deranged beliefs to their sons?

"Do you think the part about the demon could be a story? A way to explain why these spirits try to hurt people?"

Lukas took a leather journal out of the glove compartment. At least it looked like it had been a journal once. Now it was falling apart, scraps and torn pages slipping out from between the scratched covers. He opened it, tucking the loose pages back into their proper places, and handed it to me. "I wish it was just a story."

The spine was broken, the ink completely streaked in some places and illegible in others. Faded script from another time stared back at me.

"Is this Latin?"

"Yeah." Lukas pointed to the clearer print below the passage. "That's the translation."

Konstantin Lockhart
13th December 1776

After careful examination of the grimoire, we have selected the demon most suited to aid us in this mission. Andras, the Author of Discords, one who breeds distrust and dissension among men. In two nights' time, we shall summon Andras, using the angel Anarel to control him, and command the beast to find the Illuminati and destroy it from within.

May the black dove always carry you.

The rest of the page was obscured by water stains, and the back revealed nothing but a few unfamiliar symbols.

"Is there more?"

"In mine." Jared took a journal out of his jacket and dropped it in my lap. It was smaller, with black leather peeling around the edges. Loose pages were falling out of this one, too. But the handwriting was different.

Markus Lockhart
15th December 1776

Despite careful precautions, our mission has failed. We marked our skin with the demon's seal to bind him once summoned. I inscribed the seal on the floor of the church myself. Each line had to be precise. If only we had known that one was not.

We called the demon Andras, but our strength was no match for a marquis of hell. There was no will beyond his own, his only desire to kill us and open the gates of hell. A single error has unleashed an evil greater than all the sins of man. We were foolish to think we could control a beast so powerful, even with the aid of Anarel. Now her blood is on our hands.

"I don't understand. Did Andras kill the angel?" I couldn't believe I was asking the question. But the faded script, strange hand-drawn symbols, and fingerprints on the yellowed pages made the story seem more plausible.

Lukas leaned against the seat, his shoulders sagging. "No one knows. We only have bits and pieces of the journals and the story. All we know is that the Legion found a way to contain Andras."

"But once a demon gets a taste of this world, it wants more." Jared tightened his grip on the wheel, his expression dark. "Andras is settling for revenge."

"What about that book—the grimoire? Can't you use it to send him back?"

"Nobody knows what happened to it," Lukas said.

"You're saying there's no way to stop him?"

Jared shook his head. "At this point, it's damage control. We have to destroy the vengeance spirits Andras controls, so they can't do his dirty work."

I realized what they were saying. "You don't mean the two of you—"

Lukas cut me off. "Konstantin and Markus were cousins, and they each chose a blood relative to take their place. So two people from our family have always been in the Legion. Right now, those two people are Jared and me."

He couldn't be serious, not after what I'd witnessed at my house. "Your parents let you exorcise ghosts? Isn't there a minimum age requirement or something?"

"Our parents are dead." Jared tensed, but his voice didn't betray a hint of emotion.

My throat went dry at the sound of the word and the thought of any more dead parents. "I'm sorry. But shouldn't someone else do it? It's obviously dangerous."

Jared turned down an alley flanked by warehouses with dented metal doors. "There's no one else. It's our job."

"Your job?" He made it sound like they were delivering pizza.

Lukas watched me with the intense blue eyes he and his brother shared. "It's what we do, Kennedy. Our father chose Jared, and our uncle chose me. We've been training since we were kids."

"Somebody has to do it." Jared seemed almost apologetic. "If it weren't for us, you'd be dead."

Like my mom.

My chest tightened, and I took a trembling breath. "Stop the car."

"What's wrong?" Lukas asked.

I gripped the edge of the seat, my nails digging into the leather. "Please."

"Are you gonna be sick?" Jared sounded worried as he guided the van to one side of the alley.

Lukas slid out and held the door open as I stumbled onto the filthy street. I turned my back on them and focused on the shiny puddles of water in the potholes, fighting the tears burning my eyes.

"Kennedy?" I caught a glimpse of Jared's army jacket.

I spun around, shaking. "My mom is dead because of a demon your family summoned."

Jared took a step back as if I had slapped him. "Our family didn't do it alone. Someone from your family was there, too."

8. PROOF

I heard the words, but they felt impossible.

Someone from your family was there, too.

And there was no one to confirm or deny it. My aunt was the only family I had left. If one of our ancestors was in a secret society, my mom would never have told her. They barely spoke, and when they did, it always ended in an argument.

I swallowed hard, fighting to keep my voice steady. "How do you know?"

Lukas pushed past his brother, walking toward me slowly like he was approaching a frightened animal. "There are always five members of the Legion. A month ago, all five died on the same night. Exactly the same way. Our dad and uncle, your mom—"

Jared leaned against the side of the van, his hands shoved in his pockets. "You weren't the only one with a psychotic cat."

"You think this is funny?" I snapped.

"No, I didn't mean—" Jared's eyes dropped to the ground.

"I get that this is a lot to take in, but you need to know the truth," Lukas said.

I only nodded.

"Our place isn't far." Lukas led me to the van, and I climbed in without arguing. "It's not like you can go back to your house."

I hesitated for a second. "Wait. What time is it?"

"Eleven. Why?"

I was supposed to meet Elle at nine thirty. She would've gone by my house when I didn't show up. I tried to picture exactly how it looked when we left—the door blown off the hinges, windows shattered, knives sticking out of the kitchen walls. Considering the number of people who had been opening their doors when we drove away, the police had probably beaten her there.

The police meant a call to my aunt, who would have me on the next plane to Boston if I went back.

If Lukas and Jared were telling the truth, a plane ride wouldn't stop vengeance spirits from finding me. I couldn't risk leaving until I knew how to protect myself.

I turned to Lukas. "I have to make a call. I was supposed to meet my friend, and she's probably freaking out."

He handed me his cell phone. "You can't say anything about us. We don't want to deal with the cops."

"I just want to tell her that I'm okay." I dialed Elle's number, and she picked up on the first ring.

"Hello?"

"Elle—"

"Kennedy? Oh my god! Where are you?" She was talking so fast I could hardly understand her. "Your house is totally trashed and—"

"Elle? Are you alone?"

"Yeah, why?" Her usual confidence was gone.

"You can't tell anyone I'm on the phone. Do you hear me?"

"Okay."

I took a deep breath and tried to sound calm for her benefit. "Listen. I'm fine. Something happened at my house and these guys helped me."

"What *guys*?" she hissed under her breath. "Everyone is looking for you. Your house is a crime scene, and I found Elvis wandering around in the street."

"You found him? Is he all right?"

"Your stupid cat's fine. He's in my car." Her voice rose, hysteria taking over. "But I'm in the parking lot at the police station. I practically had to tell them everything you ate for the last two days. They think you were abducted."

"Hold on." I hit Mute and turned to Lukas. "The police think someone kidnapped me. Should she tell them I'm okay?"

"No," he said quickly. "They'll ask her a million questions, and she might get nervous and let something slip."

I got back on the line. "Elle, you can't tell anyone you talked to me."

She sniffled. "Are you running away? Is this about boarding school? You can move in with me if you don't want to go."

It killed me to scare her like this. "I'm not running away. It has to do with what happened to my mom."

"Her heart attack? Sometimes those things just—"

"She didn't die of a heart attack." The words felt different when I said them out loud. Truer.

For a second, Elle didn't respond. "What are you talking about?"

Lukas gestured for me to hurry up.

"I have to go."

"Call me back," she whispered desperately.

"I will." I hung up, wishing she was here and grateful she wasn't at the same time.

Jared pulled away from the curb, and Lukas' journal slipped off the seat. I picked it up and ran my hand over the worn cover. My mom's silver bracelet slid down my wrist. "I wish I had something like this that belonged to my mom."

She would've known what to do in this situation. I missed sitting on the counter while she cooked, complaining about school and guys and the current drawing that wasn't meeting my standards. My mom always had the answers, or at least the brownies.

Lukas tucked the loose pages inside the book. "I inherited it when my uncle died. Every member of the Legion records their experiences in a journal and passes it down to the person who replaces them. Your mom probably had one, too."

They still believed she was one of them—that her attack wasn't random, but retribution for our ancestors' involvement in summoning a demon over two hundred years ago.

It was probably the reason they hadn't left me back at my house. "She wasn't a member of the Legion."

Jared rubbed the back of his neck. "Your mother died exactly like the other members, and a vengeance spirit tried to kill you the same way. You need more proof than that?"

I didn't have any proof, but it made me wonder if he

did. "Was my mom's name on a list or something in one of your journals?"

Jared shifted in his seat and pretended to concentrate on the road.

"There's no list," Lukas said. "Each member of the Legion only knows the name of one other member. They don't have any information on the remaining three. It was a safety precaution to keep something like this from happening."

There was no list, nothing conclusive to link my mom to this group. They were making this up as they went along. "My mom never mentioned any of this to me, and I just finished packing everything she owned. There was no journal."

"Maybe she hid it somewhere," Jared said. "Our dad used to do that."

"Okay. Then why wasn't she training me?" I turned to Lukas, hoping he would be more reasonable. "You guys have known about all this since you were kids, right?"

"More or less." Lukas rolled the silver coin over his fingers.

"Maybe you weren't next in line," Jared offered. He had no way of knowing how cruel it sounded to me. My mother was the only family I'd ever had.

What if she had something else out there—something more than me?

With so little left to hold on to, I couldn't let myself

think that way. "There's no 'next in line.' My mom wasn't part of this. The demon must have made a mistake."

Lukas tossed the coin in the air and caught it, closing his hand around it. "The only mistake he made was leaving us alive."

We rode the rest of the way in awkward silence. I couldn't reconcile my life with the secrets Lukas and Jared were convinced it held. The all-night movie marathons and catastrophic cooking classes that left our kitchen draped in homemade pasta we never ate—those were the things my mother and I did together. There were no discussions about ancestry or religion.

My father had abandoned me, taking our shared heritage with him. I didn't know anything about him except that it destroyed my mom when he left, and I knew even less about his family. Church was equally alien, a place where my friends were trapped on Sundays while I ate chocolate chip pancakes in front of the TV. If my mom was a member of a secret society charged with protecting the world from vengeance spirits, then the world was seriously screwed.

Three unmarked streets later, Jared pulled over in an alley behind an overflowing Dumpster. Black fire escapes loomed above the doors. It looked like the kind of place where you'd find an underground club.

Why were we stopping here?

Jared grabbed a duffel bag from behind the seat and held the door open. It took me a moment to realize he was holding it for me. I climbed out, misjudging the distance between my foot and the step bar, and slipped. Jared caught my arm to steady me.

"Thanks." I smiled without thinking. Something registered in his deep blue eyes—a gentleness I hadn't seen before. It caught me off guard. But then it was gone, and he turned away without a word.

Lukas stood in front of a metal door, sorting through a bunch of keys.

Maybe this was a storage facility.

Five black dots that resembled the face of a die were spray painted above the lock, and a thick white line ran along the base of the door. It reminded me of the residue left on the streets after the snowplows came through.

Lukas noticed me staring and pointed at the symbol. "That's a quincunx, a voodoo ward to protect the place."

I nodded as if I knew what he was talking about. "Do you keep valuable stuff here?"

He gave me a strange look. "We keep all our stuff here."

It took me a second to realize what he meant. I tried to hide my surprise, but I didn't know a lot of people who lived in warehouses.

Lukas gestured at the white line in front of the door. "Make sure you step over the salt line without breaking it. Spirits hate rock salt." After the way the girl had exploded in my bedroom, that was an understatement.

As I walked inside, I prepared myself for the possibility that we were sleeping in a rat-infested building. I couldn't have been more wrong. Exposed pipes ran along the ceiling and gray steel beams reached up from the floor. White sheets hung from a wire that ran the length of the building, dividing the enormous room into two sections.

A break between the sheets revealed four neatly made mattresses, and shelves overflowing with clothes and books. A matching couch and chairs were positioned around a coffee table littered with papers and soda cans.

The floor vibrated from some serious bass, and I followed the sound of the White Stripes' "Icky Thump" to the far end of the building.

This side of the warehouse looked like a cross between a library and a metal shop. Books rose in tall stacks along the walls, with maps and drawings of strange symbols taped above them. Another cryptic design was painted in the middle of the floor—a heptagram enclosed within a circle, with more unfamiliar symbols intricately drawn between the lines. It must have taken someone hours to sketch that kind of detail on such a massive scale.

Power tools littered every available surface—from drills and sanders to screwdrivers and table saws, their orange extension cords tangled on the floor. Gun racks covered an entire wall, but the weapons resting on them didn't look like regular guns. Most of the barrels didn't match the bodies, as if someone had welded two different firearms together.

Someone like the kid sitting behind the workbench with a soldering iron in one hand, and a weapon straight out of a science-fiction movie in the other.

A hoodie shrouded his pale features, revealing only a long strip of blond bangs. A huge pair of headphones hung around his neck, and he was so caught up in his work and the music blaring from the speakers that he didn't notice us right away. How old was he? Fourteen?

"Hey, you guys are back," he shouted over the music, pushing his protective goggles on top of his head, which only made him look younger. "Check out what I've been working on."

He held up the remains of an automatic weapon

complete with protruding bolts, crude soldering marks, and duct tape wrapped around the handle. The tape must've been his trademark.

Please be normal.

But what were the odds? The kid was building guns like they were model cars.

"Can you turn that down?" Lukas yelled, pointing at the speakers.

"No problem." The boy leaned back and spun a dial behind him. He grinned at me and tossed the gun, or whatever it was, on the table. "You found her."

What was he talking about?

Jared dropped the duffel bag and his shoulders relaxed. He lifted the weapon off the table and nodded his approval. "Looks good."

Lukas gestured at the kid. "Kennedy, this is Priest. Engineer, inventor, mechanic, and a few other things we haven't figured out yet."

Priest flashed an impish grin. "Technically I'm a genius, but I prefer jack-of-all-trades. It sounds cooler. What's your specialty, Kennedy?"

"My specialty?" I was pretty sure he wasn't referring to my grilled cheese.

"You know, combat and weapons like Jared or mechanical engineering like me? What's your poison?"

Combat and weapons? Was he kidding? I'd never seen

a gun before last night, when Lukas and Jared showed up in my room. Now I was staring at dozens of them.

Priest waited for me to impress him with a mind-blowing talent I didn't possess. Drawing didn't seem on the same level as weapons and engineering.

"Umm..."

Lukas walked over and clamped his free hand on Priest's shoulder, giving it an affectionate squeeze. "We'll get to that later. Kennedy's probably beat. We had a run-in with a poltergeist at her place."

Priest's eyes widened. "For real? What happened? Spill."

Lukas recounted the story while Priest hung on every word. He wanted all the details. Exactly how powerful was it? How close did the knives come to hitting us? I couldn't believe his reaction. The kid was completely fascinated by a situation that would've terrified most people, including me.

Jared took a black metal toolbox down from the top of the fridge and sat on the floor, waving me over. I hesitated until he opened the box and I noticed the medical supplies inside.

"How old is he?" I whispered, tilting my head in Priest's direction.

"Fifteen."

"How old are you?"

"Seventeen," Jared answered without looking at me.

I waited for him to ask me the same question. "Don't you want to know how old I am?"

"I already know we're the same age." They probably had some kind of file on me, full of information I didn't want them to know. Jared took out a bottle of peroxide and some gauze. "Let me see your hands."

I held them up and wiggled my fingers. "They're fine."

"Really?" Jared rotated my wrist gently, revealing a trail of bloody scrapes across my palm. I tried to ignore the way my skin tingled in the places where his fingers touched. Resting my hand on his leg, he started to work the tiny bits of gravel out of my skin. He was so gentle that I barely felt it.

Not what I would've expected from a guy who was heavily armed and always so serious.

I stared at his long eyelashes. In any high school, the girls would be lining up for him. Was he in school before his father died? I wanted to ask, but it felt too personal while our hands were touching like this.

I settled for something else. "What did Priest mean when he asked about my specialty?"

"The original members of the Legion were experts in different areas—symbology, weaponry, alchemy, mathematics, engineering—and those specialties have been passed down," he said. "They've probably changed a little in a couple hundred years, but you get the idea."

"More proof that I'm not a member, and neither was my

mom. I don't have any talents except drawing, and my mother spent all her time cooking." I tried to sound casual as he finished wrapping my hand. "So unless vengeance spirits are into art or baked goods, you've got the wrong girl."

Jared pressed the last piece of tape against my palm with his thumbs. He lifted his head slowly and his eyes met mine. "I don't think you're the wrong girl."

I knew he wasn't talking about me the way a regular boy might, but it felt like he was.

"Priest said your area of expertise is combat and weapons?"

He examined the excessive amount of tape crisscrossing the bandage. "It's definitely not first aid."

I pretended to inspect his work, my skin still tingling from his touch. "What does that mean exactly?"

Lukas walked over and stepped in front of his brother, staring down at him. "It means Jared can kick some serious ass."

Jared seemed uncomfortable. He tossed what was left of the tape into the toolbox and stood up, disappearing behind the worktable without a word. Lukas took his brother's place on the floor next to me. They looked so much alike that it almost felt like Jared was still sitting there.

"What's your specialty?" I asked, filling the awkward silence.

"Patterns."

"You lost me."

Lukas laughed, and I noticed a subtle physical difference between the two brothers. They had exactly the same intense blue eyes and long, straight lashes, but when Lukas smiled, his eyes opened up like a break in the clouds. The storm in Jared's never parted.

"Areas with an increase in paranormal activity have certain patterns—electrical storms, severe weather fluctuations, dramatic increases in suicide and violent crime. My job is to find those patterns, which usually involves hacking into the mainframes at hospitals, news stations, and police departments." He sounded almost apologetic. "It's not as cool as combat and weapons, but we don't get to pick our specialties. We inherit them from the Legion member who chooses us."

Lukas' eyes dropped to the ground.

"Hacking computers sounds pretty cool to me," I said.

"When I was a kid, my dad sparred with me all the time. He even taught me how to take his guns apart and make salt rounds. I thought he wanted me to replace him. But when the time came, he picked Jared."

I wondered if that was the source of the tension between Lukas and Jared, a father picking one son over the other. Judging by the strained expression on Lukas' face, it was at least one reason.

"Analyzing that kind of information seems complicated. Maybe your father knew that you were better at it."

"You sound like my dad." He forced a smile. "It's not all analysis. I destroy my share of vengeance spirits, too."

"Not tonight." A girl's voice echoed through the room, deep and authoritative. "You need to hit the books and find the Marrow."

A tall girl towered over us, arms crossed tightly over her chest.

"Your wish is my command," Lukas teased. He stood up and offered me a hand. "Kennedy, this is Alara."

She didn't strike me as particularly friendly, wearing what resembled authentic military-issue cargo pants, a leather tool belt, and a T-shirt that read TAKE NO PRISONERS. But that wasn't what threw me. The girl was beautiful— with long wavy hair, perfectly smooth caramel-colored skin, and dark almond-shaped eyes. The silver hoop in her eyebrow made her look even more formidable.

Alara gave me the once-over, evaluating me on criteria I probably didn't meet. "So you're the mysterious fifth member?"

"I'm not—"

"It was a close call," Lukas interrupted. "We got there just in time."

"That's what you get for having cats." Alara frowned at me, an expression her features settled into easily. "Do you know how many cultures have folklore about cats stealing people's breath?"

I didn't.

"But how often has it actually happened?" Lukas asked offhandedly. The color drained from his face immediately.

Alara raised her eyebrows. "This month? That would be five." She ticked off our murdered family members one at a time on her fingers.

I turned to Lukas. "Why would you have a cat if you knew that was possible?"

"They can see spirits, which makes them a convenient warning system," he said. "Up until now, the whole cats-killing-people-in-their-sleep thing was more of an urban legend."

"You didn't have a cat?" I asked Alara.

Her frown deepened and she touched the silver medal around her neck, bearing yet another symbol I didn't recognize. "My grandmother was Haitian. She knew better. The cat must've climbed through an open window."

The more I learned about the invisible world lurking around us, the more I wanted to be oblivious again. But it was too late for that. Until I found a way to convince these people, and a demon, that I wasn't the fifth member of their secret exorcist society, my life was in danger.

"Wait." Alara stared at me, eyes wide, as the realization settled over her. "Are you messing with me?"

Any answer I gave her would be the wrong one.

"She doesn't know anything about the Legion," Lukas

said, before I had a chance to respond. "No one ever told her."

A shudder ran through her body. "Oh my god."

She knew what I was now—what I had been all along. A liability.

10. THE MARROW

Lukas studied a creased US map spread over the coffee table, while everyone else flipped through a stack of newspapers on the floor. I hadn't been at the warehouse long, and Alara's plan to hit the books was already in full force.

I leaned over the map. "What are you looking for?"

"See this?" Lukas pointed to the red circles drawn around various cities and towns: Johnstown, Pennsylvania; Salem, West Virginia; Sugarcreek, Ohio; Wilmington, Delaware; Washington, DC. "I tracked paranormal surges over the last month and all these places had serious activity. We were looking for you, but I realized there was a pattern based on the other cities we checked first."

It never occurred to me that they had looked anywhere else. "How did you figure out where I lived?"

"Hacked into local police servers and cross-referenced the cities with surges against death records. I looked for kids about our age that had parents who died the same night as the other members of the Legion. Then we took a road trip."

I couldn't believe they had worked so hard to find me. "What about school?"

Priest glanced up from the newspaper, headphones covering his ears. "Homeschooled. The public education system in Northern California wasn't equipped to meet my needs."

Jared shrugged. "We didn't live in the best neighborhood in Philadelphia. No one really cared if you showed up at school. We traveled with our dad a lot, so we weren't there much anyway."

Alara ripped an article out of the newspaper in her lap. "I just bailed. Girls' school sucks."

With her combat boots, eyebrow ring, and chipped silver nail polish, she looked more like art school material. My hand itched at the thought of drawing.

Lukas traced the perimeter of the circled cities with his finger. "I think the Marrow might be somewhere in here."

"What's the Marrow?"

"It's the location of Andras' power supply in our world. Sort of like his personal supernatural power plant," he explained. "Demons gain strength by taking control of human souls—either temporarily while we're alive, or permanently after we die. The more souls they control, the more powerful they become."

Priest jumped in. "But Andras is trapped between his world and ours. He can't cross over and possess people, or draft them into his ranks when they die. He has to settle for influencing vengeance spirits and using them to cause violence and suffering."

"Which creates more vengeance spirits he can control," Lukas added.

I imagined hundreds of battered souls like the girl in my bedroom lined up in a row, ready for battle.

Priest unscrewed the faceplate on a device that resembled an old transistor radio. "The bigger the surges in paranormal activity, the closer we are to the Marrow. At least, that's what my granddad used to say."

He stopped working and stared at his hands. Priest's grandfather must've been the member of the Legion he had replaced. It was easy to forget that I wasn't the only one who had lost someone.

Lukas noticed Priest's reaction and messed up the younger boy's hair. Priest swatted his arm, the beginning of a smile tugging at the corners of his mouth.

"If we find the Marrow, we can take out the spirits Andras controls," Jared said. "And cut off his power supply."

"Will that get rid of him?" I asked.

The four of them looked at one another.

Lukas shook his head. "No. But it will make him a lot weaker. Damage control, remember?"

I listened as they strategized, trying to make sense of the surges and the red circles. The warehouse was only an hour from my house in Georgetown, but it felt worlds away.

I needed to talk to someone who wasn't tracking paranormal activity or searching for a demon's hideout. "Lukas, can I use your phone again?"

Alara snapped to attention. "She can't call anyone."

"Don't worry." Lukas raised a hand to reassure her. "She just wants to check in with her friend."

"Her friend?" Alara gasped. "Are you insane?"

"My number's blocked. I doubt her friend knows how to trace a call."

"What if she tells someone where we are?" Alara was talking about me like I wasn't there.

"I wouldn't do that," I said. "But if I don't call, she'll try to find me."

Lukas handed me his cell. "It's fine. Just be careful what you say."

I slipped between the sheets suspended from the ceiling and sat down next to the fridge, where Jared had bandaged my hand.

The phone only rang once before Elle picked up. "Hello?"

My whole body seemed to relax when I heard her voice. "It's me."

87

"Where are you? I'm totally freaking out."

I didn't know where to begin. Elle had never doubted me before, but demons were a lot to dump on anyone. "I need to tell you something, and it's going to sound crazy."

"I'm fine with crazy."

It was like ripping off a Band-Aid. The only way to do it was fast. "I saw a ghost."

"You saw your mom?" She didn't sound surprised.

"No—" I hesitated. "It was the ghost of a dead girl. I saw her in the cemetery one night and then again in my room."

I waited for her to rattle off a list of the symptoms of depression.

"Is that why you ran away?"

This was the hard part. "The ghost killed my mom, and it tried to kill me. I know it sounds completely insane, but it's true."

Please believe me.

I held my breath, waiting for her to say something.

"Is that who trashed your house? The ghost?" It was the same matter-of-fact tone Elle used when she grilled me about the latest social scandal at school. She wanted the details, which meant she believed me.

"You don't think I'm losing it?"

She sighed dramatically. "I've watched *Paranormal Encounters*. I'm not a total idiot. So was it the ghost or what?"

"No, it was...something a little different."

"Did you dig up a graveyard?" Her voice rose, and I could practically see her yelling at the phone.

"I don't really understand everything, but the guys I'm with do."

"Who are these guys, anyway?"

I wasn't willing to start talking salt rounds and secret societies. I was already pushing it. "They track violent spirits and destroy them."

"Like the ghostbusters?"

"More like exorcists."

Her bedsprings groaned, the way they did whenever she fell back onto her bed. "Please tell me you aren't possessed."

I almost laughed. "I'm not. But the spirits are dangerous, and I need these guys to help me get rid of them."

"How many guys are we talking about?" She perked up.

"Three, but one of them is only fifteen." I could see the wheels spinning in her mind. "There's another girl here, too."

"When are you coming back?"

My throat tightened. "I don't know. But you can't tell anyone you talked to me. Okay?"

She didn't respond.

"Elle!"

"You know I won't say anything." She pretended to sound offended.

Alara peeked through the sheets.

"Elle, I have to go."

"Be careful," she pleaded.

"I will." I hung up and held the phone to my chest, wondering how long it would be until I saw her again.

When I came back, the four of them were packing it in for the night. I handed Lukas his phone and straightened the stacks of newspapers. I didn't want to look completely useless.

Jared tipped his chin toward a mattress in the corner. "You can take my bed. I like the couch."

"No, it's okay—"

"I like the couch," he repeated more firmly.

I was too tired to argue—and too cold. The warehouse was freezing, and I still didn't have a jacket. I rubbed my hands over my arms.

Priest noticed and tossed me a hoodie from his shelf. "You'll need it. This place is a meat locker."

As I slid my arms into the sleeves and lay down on the bed, I relaxed for what felt like the first time in days—until I noticed Jared coming back.

Maybe he'd changed his mind about letting me have his bed.

I started to get up when he pointed at the pillows. "Mind if I take one?"

"Sure—I mean no."

He held up his hands, and his T-shirt slid up, exposing a few inches of skin above the waistband of his jeans. My cheeks grew warm and I tossed him the pillow, hoping he wouldn't notice. He stood there for a moment as if he wanted to say something, but then he walked away.

It was a sharp contrast to the crooked smile Lukas gave me as he flopped down on the mattress across from mine. His fingers flew over the controls of a video game. He noticed me watching him. "It's Tetris."

"He plays it all the time." Alara walked by and rolled her eyes, twisting her hair into a loose knot.

Lukas didn't look up from the screen. "It requires hard-core spatial skills and pattern recognition."

"I'm sure it does," she said sarcastically.

Priest laughed and closed his eyes, still wearing his headphones, as Jared stretched out on the couch. It seemed like he was on the opposite side of a boundary no one could cross.

I wondered what had happened to Jared—who had hurt him. But his walls were even higher than mine.

Alara switched off the lights. I listened to the muffled music from Priest's headphones and the pinging sound of Tetris, wishing I could turn off my thoughts as easily.

I was lying on a mattress in a warehouse with four people I barely knew—four people who seemed to know more about my life than I did. Was it possible they knew more about my mom, too?

My eyes burned and I felt the tears building, but I didn't want to let myself cry. If I started, I might not be able to stop.

The music and video game sounds finally faded, blanketing the room in silence. I slipped through the sheets and tiptoed to the other side of the warehouse where the gun racks and shelves of ammo were silhouetted in the darkness. Evidence of how unprepared I was for everything that was happening to me.

I was safe now, but I couldn't stay here forever.

Tears slid down my neck before I realized they were falling.

I sat on the floor next to Priest's worktable and buried my face in my knees. I cried quietly, choking back sobs until my throat was raw.

"Kennedy?" Someone whispered my name.

I covered my face with my hands.

"Want to talk about it?" It was Lukas or Jared, but his voice was so quiet I couldn't tell which one. I shook my head, tears running through the spaces between my fingers.

He sat down next to me, and I could smell the salt and copper on his skin.

"I know this is hard. I lost it when my dad died, and I didn't know how we were gonna do this without him." He spoke slowly, his voice gentle and soothing. I realized it was Lukas, sharing something painful to make me feel better.

"I wish I could take it back." He hesitated. "I mean, change things."

I took a ragged breath, and he touched my back gently.

"Hey, will you look at me?"

I shook my head. I couldn't stop crying, and I didn't want him to see me falling apart.

"I get it," he whispered, so close I could feel his breath on my neck. "I don't think I would've made it without Luke."

I froze.

Lukas wasn't the one with his hand on my back.

It was Jared, the boy who barely spoke, the one who seemed so distant.

I don't know how long we stayed that way. Eventually, I ran out of tears, and Jared took my hand and led me through the warehouse. I climbed in his bed, and he retreated to the couch without a word. But I could still smell the salt on his skin.

11. OPHTHALMIC SHIFT

When I woke up, Lukas, Jared, and Alara were hunched over the map again. After an hour of skimming articles for unusual weather patterns and bizarre accounts of unexplained events, I'd learned a few things about surges and paranormal activity. My mind had also taken hundreds of mental snapshots—from neglected houses and morbid crime scenes to used car ads—each one sorted and cataloged automatically.

On Marrow overload, I offered to be Priest's assistant for a while. He was determined to design the Big Bad of vengeance spirit hunting weapons to take down whatever Andras had waiting for them.

"Hold this." Priest handed me his blowtorch.

"I don't think—"

"It's totally safe. Unless you turn it on."

Like I know how to do that?

"We need some serious firepower." Priest scanned his journal for old designs he could tweak.

Alara stalked in wearing loose cargos and a fitted tank that showed off her muscular arms. She grabbed a box of Pop-Tarts off Priest's shelf and threw me a perfunctory glance from under her mascaraed lashes before disappearing again.

"Alara seems nice," I said once she was out of earshot.

"Ah…are we talking about the same person?"

I laughed. "What's her specialty? Aside from intimidation?"

"Wards. Her grandmother was a voodoo priestess or something. I forget what they're called. But Alara's pretty badass."

Badass and gorgeous. Great.

Priest gestured at the journal and headed for the fridge. "Keep looking."

Turning the pages carefully, something caught my eye—a tiny symbol hidden in one of the designs. I'd seen it before.

Priest came back carrying two sodas.

"What's this?" I pointed at the sketch.

He glanced at the page. "Some kind of ocular device."

"Why does it have Andras' seal on it?"

"What are you talking about?" He leaned over, and I

pointed at the symbol. Priest dropped the cans, and soda exploded all over the floor.

Lukas stuck his head between the sheets. "What are you two doing?"

Priest gazed at the page, transfixed. "Get everyone in here. Now."

They crowded around the worktable to see the diagram—a mechanical cylinder with the words *Ophthalmic Shift* printed in tight script at the top.

"Is it one of your grandfather's inventions?" Jared leaned over my shoulder and examined the drawing. I remembered the way his hand had felt on my back as I cried, and the way he had smelled—the same way he smelled now. I edged forward, trying to put some space between us.

Priest shook his head. "That's not my granddad's handwriting, and this sketch is really old."

A piece of clear glass was cut into one end like a window. Five looping symbols were etched around the outside. There were four other components—silver disks, each embedded with a different shade of glass: blue, red, yellow, and green. According to the diagram, the disks slid into the middle of the cylinder like trays.

Alara twisted her eyebrow ring. "What is it?"

"An ocular device," Priest said.

"In English?" Jared leaned closer.

Priest tapped the top of the cylinder on the page. "You

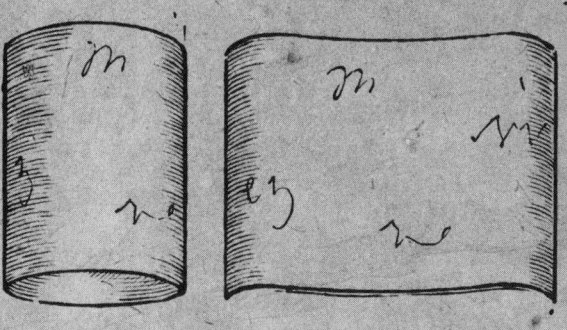

Ophthalmic
Shift

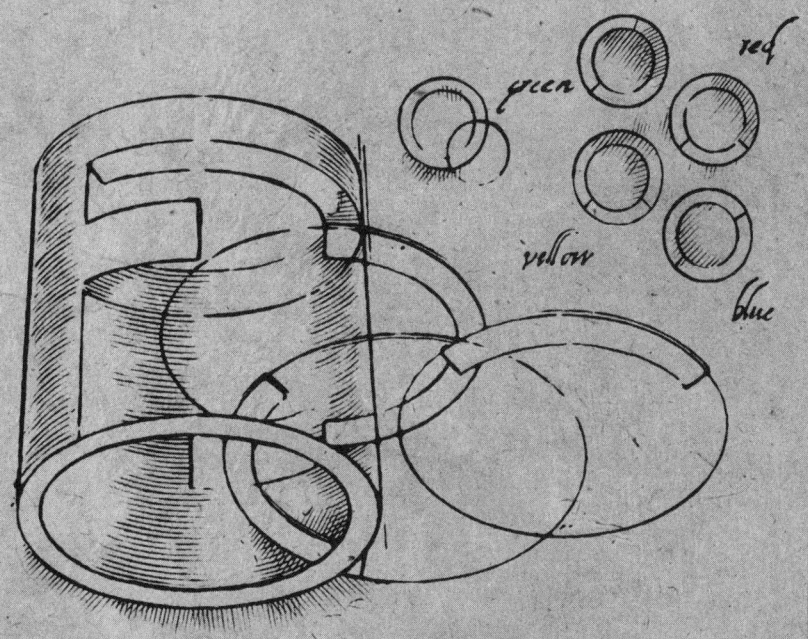

green

red

yellow

blue

Lilburn

look through here and each piece of colored glass inside allows you to see a different layer of the infrared spectrum—things you can't see with the naked eye. The way a black light picks up the color white and amplifies it."

"Are you saying it's a decryption device?" Lukas asked.

How did he make that jump?

Priest nodded. "A pretty sophisticated one, considering it's completely mechanical. If you used the right type of ink, you could write on almost anything and no one would be able to see it without these disks. If someone knew what they were doing, they could actually design a written code that required all five pieces to decipher."

Lukas froze. "Five pieces?"

"Yeah—" Priest started, but Lukas was halfway across the room.

"Luke?" Jared called after him. His brother didn't even break stride, and I felt Jared's body tense behind me.

"And you never noticed that picture before?" Alara asked before an awkward silence set in.

Priest gave her a hard stare. "Of course I did. But there are hundreds of sketches in here. And like I said, that isn't my granddad's handwriting. His is down in the corner." The word *Lilburn* was printed neatly at the bottom of the page. "Another member of the Legion must have drawn it before he inherited the journal."

"Then why is this Shift thing such a big deal all of a sudden?" Jared asked.

"Because of this." Priest pointed at the seal. "Kennedy found it."

Alara and Jared squinted to see what had taken my mind only seconds to record in complete detail. They gasped as recognition registered on their faces.

Jared looked at me. "How'd you even see it?"

"I have twenty-twenty vision." I didn't want to tell them about my freakish memory. Priest might think it was cool, but Alara would undoubtedly point out that it wasn't very useful, unless we needed to take a standardized test about destroying vengeance spirits.

"If the seal is there, it means something," Alara said.

"It does." Lukas parted the sheet with one hand, his journal in the other. "Listen to this. 'Five pieces. Separated until the day comes when, united, we can finally destroy him. Until that day, the pieces remain hidden from the demon that hunts them. The shift is the key.' My uncle read it to me once. He thought it was a metaphor, and the five pieces represented the five members of the Legion, like the pieces of a puzzle."

"But it mentions the Shift from the drawing," I said.

Lukas set his journal on the worktable so the rest of us could see it. "The word *shift* isn't capitalized here. He didn't think it was a physical object."

"'Until the day comes when, united, we can finally destroy him.'" Alara repeated the words, trying to work it out.

"What if—?" Lukas leaned over the diagram. He gripped the sides of the table until his knuckles turned white. He finally raised his eyes to meet ours.

"I think the Shift is a weapon."

A *weapon to destroy a demon.*

The words and their implication settled around us.

"If the Shift is a weapon, why didn't the Legion use the Shift to destroy Andras?" I asked.

Priest paced in front of the table. "Maybe it was designed before they knew where to find him."

"That's a big maybe."

No one responded. They weren't going to listen to the girl who didn't even know spirits existed until two strangers shot one in her bedroom.

Alara turned to Jared, waiting for his reaction. "You really think there's a way to destroy Andras?"

"If our dad were here, he'd say—"

"There's always a way." Lukas cut him off, an edge in his voice. "You just have to find it."

Alara pointed at the word scrawled in the corner of the page. "Does *Lilburn* mean anything to you?"

Priest shook his head. "Nope."

"We need to figure out who or what Lilburn is," she said. "And if this Shift exists, we need to find it."

Lukas reached for his laptop. "Already on the first part."

When he turned it around moments later, a Gothic mansion with a peaked roof filled the screen. A medieval tower rose up on one side, the stone battlements at odds with the style of the house. The headline read *Haunted History Returns to Lilburn Mansion.*

"It's in Ellicott City." Lukas kept reading. "This iron trader, Henry Hazlehurst, built the house in 1857, and his wife and three kids died there. No written accounts of hauntings until 1923, when the new owner tore down the tower and built another one after a fire. But get this. It was completely different from the original."

Priest whistled. "That'll do it. Spirits aren't fans of construction."

Lukas scrolled farther down the page. "That's an understatement."

"Mind sharing with the rest of us?" Jared asked.

"If you give me a minute," Lukas snapped. "We don't need to make any more mistakes."

Jared's back stiffened. The tension between them stretched like a rubber band about to snap. "You mean I don't."

"What does it say?" Alara stepped between them, and Lukas focused his attention back to the article.

"Lilburn's always been haunted. Footsteps in the tower, a baby crying, a little girl playing in the hall—the usual stuff."

"That's the usual stuff?" The four of them shared a vocabulary that was completely alien to me.

"If we're dealing with a residual haunting," Priest said. I gave him a blank stare. "It's like a fingerprint, energy that's left behind after someone dies traumatically. It can be a sound like footsteps, or an actual apparition. But the apparition can't interact with people because it's not really there."

"There's nothing residual about what's going on at Lilburn now." Lukas handed the laptop to his brother without looking at him.

Jared's eyes darkened. "Two people almost died there within a week. One fell down the stairs and the other from a second-story window. Both said they were pushed, but they were alone in the house when it happened."

"The name of this place is written on the same page as

the diagram of the Shift," Alara said. "What are the odds?"

It was one question we could all answer.

The White Stripes blared from the speakers behind Priest's worktable. This time it was "Seven Nation Army," and Priest looked like he was outfitting an army of his own. I checked off supplies from his list. I quizzed Priest and Alara about each piece of equipment.

Priest tossed Alara a box of nails and filled in the blanks for me. "It's like packing for a trip when you don't know what the weather will be like."

I only recognized about half of the items Alara stuffed in the bag, and I had no idea what they planned to do with any of it. But I was determined to find out.

I held up the nails. "I'm guessing these are for severe thunderstorms?"

Priest grinned. "Or unexpected rain, depending on the vengeance spirit." He handed Alara a high-tech crossbow with orange duct tape wrapped around the barrel.

"You can shoot spirits with that?"

Alara scowled. Spotting Andras' seal on the diagram had only earned me a temporary reprieve. I sensed her sizing me up every time she looked at me, trying to determine what my ignorance would cost them.

"Almost any type of weapon works as long as you have

the right ammo. Regular bullets won't hurt spirits. They just piss them off," Priest said.

"Your grandfather taught you how to make all this stuff?"

"Yeah. He could build a weapon out of a soda can." Priest examined a leather glove with spikes protruding from the knuckles. "I need to do a quick fix. Alara, put this on for a minute."

She nodded at the soldering iron. "Don't burn me."

I scanned the list while Priest lit the blue flame on the soldering iron: nail gun, crossbow, shotgun, strike gloves, nails, bolts, shells, salt, EMF detectors, batteries, flashlights, torch, headphones. I smiled at the last one and watched Priest work. I flipped over the list, and the pencil in my hand started to move, following the curves of his face, the shape of the hood flipped over his head. But his trademark headphones morphed into part of his body like a crazy steampunk helmet.

It felt good to be sketching, like I was suddenly myself again.

Priest finished and looked over. "What are you drawing?"

"You." I penciled in some quick lines to round out the sketch.

He pushed the goggles up on his forehead and walked around behind me. "Wow. That's amazing."

Alara craned her neck to get a better look and did a double take. "He's right."

"Lots of people are better." I handed him the sketch and tucked the pencil behind my ear.

"Well, I don't know any." Priest ripped off the sheet and slid it into his pocket. "I'm saving this in case you're famous one day."

If someone had said that to me a week ago, I would've holed up in my room and sketched for the rest of the day. Instead, I was hiding in a warehouse, packing ammo, just hoping to make it through another one.

13. COLD IRON

You're about to walk into a real haunted house.

With its weathered gray brick and medieval tower, Lilburn Mansion looked more like an abandoned castle from a European guidebook than the scene of paranormal attacks. Whether the spirits inside the house were under the influence of a demon or not, two people had almost died here. I wasn't studying maps and sorting weapons anymore.

I scanned the second-story windows, wondering which one the person fell from.

"You okay?" Lukas walked up beside me.

"I'm good." If I pretended it was true, maybe I would believe it.

"I was six the first time I saw a ghost." Lukas stared at the house, but I sensed him watching me. "I woke up one night, and a little girl was sitting by the window playing cat's cradle. When the moonlight hit her body, it passed right through her."

I pictured the girl with the handprints around her throat. "Were you scared?"

"I thought it was a dream until I saw her again. She was sitting in the same spot playing cat's cradle. After what felt like forever, she held up her hands with a blue string webbed between them, and she spoke to me."

"What did she say?"

" 'You have to lace your fingers just right to catch your dreams. And you don't want to lose them because they're not easy to find again.' Then she faded away like she was never there. When I woke up the next morning, the blue string was sitting on the windowsill, looped in a perfect cat's cradle."

I gasped. "I would've lost it."

"That's the weirdest part. I didn't. She was just a lonely spirit caught between worlds. I wanted you to know they aren't all bad." Lukas pulled something out of his pocket. When he uncurled his fingers, it was tangled in his palm.

A web of blue string.

"And I want you to know something else."

I couldn't take my eyes off the tangled loops.

"I'm just like you, Kennedy. There are things I want. Things that have nothing to do with destroying demons and vengeance spirits." Lukas put the string in my hand and closed my fingers around it. "So you can catch your dreams."

He knows I'm scared. It doesn't mean anything.

I held the string, and I realized the cat's cradle wasn't to catch my dreams.

It was to catch me.

⊰ • ⊱

Jared noticed us walking back down the hill and stopped unloading weapons from the van. His eyes moved from his brother to me. I started to smile, but he looked away.

Alara threw Lukas a disapproving look, like we had stayed out all night and showed up with our clothes on inside out. I pulled at my T-shirt, suddenly uncomfortable.

"How's it look up there?" Alara asked without turning around.

"Just like the picture," Lukas said.

Alara pointed at a plastic milk jug on the ground with the words *holy water* scrawled on the front. "Can you grab that?"

I didn't know if she was talking to me, but I picked it up anyway.

"Thanks." She poured some of the holy water into a plastic soda bottle.

"So that stuff really works?"

Alara slipped the bottle into the leather tool belt around her waist. "About sixty percent of the time."

She systematically filled the rest of the slots in her belt—a pouch of salt, liquid salt rounds, a black marker. It reminded me of the way Elle put on her makeup in the car without a mirror.

"How many times have you done this?" I asked.

Alara shrugged. "With these guys? Six."

Unless studying and making out in my room counted, I hadn't even been on six dates.

I wanted to ask her so many questions. Would the spirits haunting Lilburn look like the strangled girl from my room? Would they be as easy to destroy? Lukas and Jared only had one gun the night they burst into my room. The four of them were bringing a lot more firepower this time.

"Heads up, Luke." Jared tossed his brother the crossbow followed by a ripped cardboard box. Lukas opened the box without a word and examined the pointed projectiles. They looked more like long bullets than like arrows.

"Cool, huh?" Priest said. "Cold-iron bolts. I made them a few days ago."

"Why does the iron need to be cold?" I asked.

"That's what they call it when you hammer iron into shape without heating it." Priest opened a box of nails and loaded a nail gun. "Spirits hate the stuff. It destroys them or burns like hell, depending on how strong they are."

"Got it." I pointed at the nails scattered around him. "Cold iron?"

"You're catching on."

Lukas loaded the remaining bolts and filled one of his pockets with salt. His cuff slid up and a thin layer of salt dusted his wrist. There was a black design on his skin.

"Is that a tattoo?" I asked.

Priest glanced at Lukas.

Lukas followed my eyes to his wrist and pulled down his sleeve. "It's nothing."

"So what's the plan?" Priest asked as he handed Jared the nail gun.

Jared dumped a handful of nails into the pocket of his army jacket. "Lukas and Alara can check out the house. We'll take the tower."

"Let me guess? I can monitor the paranormal activity." Priest sounded disappointed.

Jared checked the trigger on the weapon. "It's an important job."

Priest shoved a handheld device that looked like a radio into one of his back pockets and tucked a calculator in the other.

"Planning to do your math homework in the haunted house?" I teased.

Priest perked up. "I wouldn't need one for my homework, but they're good for lots of other stuff." He walked over and stood beside Jared. Lukas and Alara were already standing together.

"Who am I going with?" I asked.

The four of them looked at one another. No one reacted except Priest, who immediately put on his headphones.

"Nobody," Jared finally answered. "You're staying here."

Andras was responsible for my mother's death. If there was a weapon capable of destroying him, I wanted to help them find it. "I'm going with you."

Jared pushed past me without a word and disappeared around the side of the van.

I was right on his heels. "You think if you ignore me, I'll just wait out here? I don't care—"

He whipped around. "I'm not letting you go in that house."

"It's not your decision to make."

Jared's eyes clouded over and met mine. "It is if there's a vengeance spirit in there...."

"You've been trying to convince me that this is my destiny or my duty, or whatever your parents told you guys to make you trade a normal life for *this*." I yanked on the pocket of his jacket, the nails rattling inside. "If I'm really one of you, shouldn't I see what I'm up against?"

Anger flickered in his eyes. "My *parents* didn't tell me

anything. My mom died ten minutes after she gave birth to us. And my dad told me the truth. Can you say the same thing?"

I bit the inside of my cheek.

Jared's voice dropped. "You don't get to judge my father or my life. What we do is important. It means something."

I wanted to fire back with a comment that would hurt him the way he'd tried to hurt me, but I couldn't. No matter how different we were, Jared and I shared a common denominator as uncommon as they came.

"I'm sorry. I shouldn't have—" My hands were shaking.

Jared noticed and his expression softened. "I didn't mean to yell at you. Why do you really want to go in?"

Because I wasn't just hunting vengeance spirits. If the four of them were right, I was following the path my mom left behind, the one she hid from me for reasons I might never know. I had so many questions I needed to answer.

Was she really a member of the Legion?

And the question I didn't even want to ask myself.

Am I?

Jared's eyes searched mine, and it felt like he could see the fears I was fighting so hard to hide.

"You have to do exactly what I tell you in there."

I nodded, too nervous to say anything.

When we came back around the side of the van, everyone was waiting. I knew they had probably overheard our entire conversation. Priest tried to act busy for my benefit, but Alara looked right at me.

You okay? Lukas mouthed.

I smiled weakly.

"Are we going to hang out here all day or what?" Alara stalked over to Priest's duffel bag. She pulled out the heavy leather glove with the cold-iron spikes and slipped it on.

114

"Let's go." Lukas slung the crossbow over his shoulder.

I reached for the nail gun.

"No," they said practically in unison.

"I can't go in empty-handed. That can't be safe."

"You're right." Jared climbed into the van and came out with something I actually recognized.

"You want me to wear a bulletproof vest? Are the ghosts going to shoot me?"

"It won't stop bullets, just vengeance spirits. Priest rigged it." Jared handed it to me, and my shoulder almost jerked out of the socket when he let go.

"Are you serious? This thing must weigh fifty pounds."

"I replaced the Kevlar fibers with cold-iron pellets." Priest shrugged. "They weigh a little more. I'm still working out the kinks."

I dropped the vest in the dirt.

"I'm good," I said, wishing it were true.

Priest took Lilburn's front steps two at a time and waved the handheld device around the door. "I've got nothing out here."

"Did he make that thing?" I asked Alara.

"It's an electromagnetic field meter," she answered. "He didn't make it, but I'm sure he tweaked it. Priest doesn't trust anything he didn't design." She pulled out one of her own, a rectangular device with a band of numbers running along the top and a needle at the end. "Spirits give off electromagnetic energy we can't sense. EMFs measure it."

"I probably need one, too."

Alara handed me a flashlight from her tool belt, with a smug smile. "Rule number one: only carry things you know how to use."

Even if I had to walk inside with nothing but a plastic flashlight and the knowledge I'd picked up from watching bad horror movies, I was still going in, whether Alara liked it or not.

I turned away, and she caught my arm.

"It was a joke." She sighed and handed me the EMF. "If that needle starts moving, there's a good chance a spirit is nearby. Consider yourself trained."

Priest leaned back, examining the upper stories. "This place is a lot bigger than it looked in the picture. You really think we can find the Shift?"

"It might not even be in there," Jared said.

Lukas walked closer to the house. "It's here. We just have to find it."

Jared waved Priest down from the porch and glanced in my direction. "Kennedy, you can check out the tower with me and Priest."

"She's coming with us," Lukas said forcefully.

Jared started to say something, then stopped. "I was trying to do you a favor, Luke. You're gonna have to baby-sit her in there."

My cheeks burned, and I stared at the scratches on the boots my mom had given me the night she died. How long before they were completely ruined?

Lukas nudged me with his shoulder. Something inside me relaxed, and a smile tugged at the corners of my mouth. "Ignore him. Jared always leaves behind a pretty high body count."

Was he talking about girls?

My smile vanished. "It's no big deal."

He touched my arm lightly when we reached the door. "Stay close, and if I tell you to get out of the house, you go. No arguments and no looking back. Understand?"

I nodded, every nerve in my body on edge.

Lukas cracked the lock with the butt of his crossbow.

The door swung open. Light poured into the entry-way, dust glittering in the stagnant air. I stepped into the hallway, heart pounding. My eyes followed the worn crimson carpet up the staircase.

The front door slammed behind us, and I spun around.

A shadow blackened the marble floor.

Lukas and Alara inched toward it slowly. I waited for a vengeance spirit to lunge at them.

The shadow didn't move.

Alara edged closer and looked up, her eyes resting on a huge crystal chandelier. "I think we're okay."

"Sorry." I felt like an idiot.

Lukas kicked one of the half-packed boxes scattered

around a velvet sofa in the living room. "Better safe than sorry, right?"

Alara rolled her eyes and ran a finger along the dusty banister. "Reminds me of my house. Minus the dirt." She zeroed in on the stained rose-colored sofa. "And the pink."

I navigated between the boxes, watching the needle on my EMF. A mirror in a gilded frame hung above the sofa, the warped glass making the room appear off kilter.

The needle didn't move as I followed them into the musty library on the other side of the staircase. Lukas stopped in the doorway.

"If I needed to hide something, this is where I'd put it."

We searched the shelves crammed with books and stranger things—beetles and butterflies in shadow boxes, dozens of clocks stopped at exactly the same time, and brass bookends depicting characters from *Alice's Adventures in Wonderland*. The Cheshire Cat smiled down from a tall shelf.

Alara lifted the Mad Hatter clutching a broken teapot. "This isn't creepy or anything."

I didn't know what was more unsettling—the perfect replica of Lilburn Mansion drowning in the thickened glitter of an old snow globe, or the image of a terrified Mad Hatter holding a broken piece of Wonderland.

"Maybe it's somewhere less obvious," I offered.

Alara glanced into the hall. "We should check upstairs. That's where all the activity was reported."

Lukas not so subtly stepped in front of me. "I'm right behind you."

The staircase rose sharply. I imagined someone reaching the last step and being pushed backward by an invisible hand. My hand tightened around the railing. When Lukas made it to the top, he grabbed my hand and pulled me onto the landing.

Six doors flanked each side of the narrow hallway. Oil portraits of women bound in layers of fabric and girls in pressed dresses, all wearing the same hopeless expression, lined the walls between them.

The EMF detector pinged.

"You got something?" The red light on Lucas' EMF blinked erratically as the needle jerked back and forth.

"Where is it?" I looked around, but didn't see anything.

"It might not be a paranormal entity," he said. "Other things can set them off—appliances, electrical wires, even water pipes in the walls. And these readings are all over the place."

Alara stopped, and we almost plowed into her. "I don't think it's an electrical wire."

I followed her eyes to the end of the hall.

A little girl in a yellow chiffon dress sat on the carpet playing with a porcelain doll. Its tangled blond hair spilled onto the floor.

As the girl rose, her body flickered like static on an old television set. She walked toward us, dragging the doll behind her by one arm. With her smooth, flushed skin, she looked nothing like the dead girl floating in my bedroom.

"Did you come to play?" The child's eyes lit up, bright and curious.

Lukas tried to push me behind him again, but my feet were rooted to the floor.

"Sure," Alara answered carefully. "What kind of games do you like?"

The child studied Lukas, her blue eyes lingering on his wrist. She acted as if she saw something more than his bare skin. The hem of her yellow dress fluttered in a non-existent wind.

The little girl's body flickered, revealing another face beneath her own. An old woman's empty eyes leered at us, her face slack and covered in scratches. Matted gray hair hung limp at her shoulders where the child's shiny blond strands had hung a moment ago.

She lifted the doll off the ground, its head dangling from the cord holding the toy together.

The old woman's scratched face flashed in front of the child's as she raised the broken doll higher. "I like the kind of games where people like *you* end up like *this*."

The wind increased and the girl's hair whipped around her. She stepped forward one shiny patent-leather Mary Jane at a time, dragging the mangled doll. The child pointed at Lukas, the rage in her voice at odds with her innocent features. "I know what you want."

Air swirled around the child, tangled blond hair lashing her face.

"We don't want anything." Lukas backed away, matching Alara step for step. "Kennedy, get out of here."

I heard the words, but my body didn't react. What if I moved and it made the spirit angrier?

"You can't have my doll!" she shrieked.

"We aren't trying to take your doll," Alara promised, clutching the silver medal around her neck.

"Liar!" the child screamed. "I know who you are. He told me you'd come."

Lukas raised the crossbow and aimed it over Alara's shoulder.

"Go!" he barked at me.

I stumbled back a few steps.

The child's face twisted into a wicked smile and her form flickered again, exposing the old woman lurking inside her.

Paintings flew off the walls, heavy frames splintering against Lukas' back. He dropped to his knees, covering his head, and the crossbow slipped out of his hand.

Carpet nails ripped out of the floor, pelting us like knives.

"Hey." Alara pointed the spiked glove at the girl. "Screw you and your doll."

The vengeance spirit's eyes widened, the yellow dress twisting in the whirlwind encircling her.

Lukas staggered to his feet and grabbed the crossbow, raising it again. The bolt flew through the air and hit the spirit square in the shoulder.

The doll slipped from her grasp and hit the floor, smashing to pieces.

The spirit's eyes darted to the broken shards of the doll. She opened her mouth and let out an inhuman wail.

A wooden side table pushed itself away from the wall and careened toward me. Time skipped as images flashed in front of me in a surreal sort of stop-motion.

Alara screaming—

Lukas lunging for me—

The flat edge of the table slamming into my stomach—

The sound of wood cracking as my back hit the railing. I felt my body falling, the smooth white ceiling above me.

"Kennedy!"

Something clamped down hard around my ankle, and my body jerked to a stop.

The floor swayed dangerously below me, pieces of the railing scattered over the smooth marble. The grip on my ankle tightened, and I felt myself being lifted. My body slid over the edge of the landing, and Lukas stared down at me.

"Lukas..." Alara's voice rose urgently, and Lukas leapt to his feet.

Alara's combat boots were positioned between me and the white Mary Janes marching down the hallway.

The spirit pointed at Lukas. "You broke my doll."

The old woman's face flashed behind the child's, and the spirit hurled her body into the air. Alara stepped in front of Lukas and cocked her arm back, cold-iron bolts protruding from the knuckles of her gloved hand. Alara waited until the spirit was practically on top of her before she plunged the iron spikes into the girl's stomach.

The vengeance spirit's eyes bulged, and she opened her mouth to scream. But there was no sound. Her body crackled in and out of focus as it hung from Alara's glove like another broken doll.

Lukas raised the crossbow for the third time and fired. The bolt struck the child-that-wasn't-a-child in the shoulder, and she exploded into a million fragments of nothing.

Then everything went black.

-≒ • ≓-

"Kennedy? Can you hear me?" Lukas crouched over me. "Talk to me."

The room came back into focus, and my thoughts stitched themselves together slowly. I pushed myself up, and Lukas rested his hand on my back for support.

Relief replaced the panic in his eyes. "Take it easy."

"I'm okay."

"No, you're not."

"Where's Alara?"

"She went to find Jared and Priest." He shook his head, tension carved into every line on his face. "When you fell, I thought..."

"I should've listened when you told me to go." I wasn't sure how to apologize for almost getting us killed. "I know this was important."

His fingers pressed lightly against the small of my back. "That's not what I was saying. Finding a piece of the Shift isn't worth what could've happened—"

"Wait? Did you find something?"

"Yeah. One of those colored glass disks from the diagram in Priest's journal." He looked over at the broken bits of the doll scattered across the floor. "It was hidden inside her doll."

"Where are the other pieces?"

"I don't know." Lukas ran his hand up my back and squeezed my shoulder gently. "Think you can walk?"

I nodded though I wasn't sure. My back felt like someone had driven a truck over it. "Give me a minute."

Lukas spread his jacket on the floor and collected what was left of the doll, tossing the shards into the center of the fabric.

"What are you doing?"

"We need to burn these. If a spirit's remains aren't destroyed, it can come back. The same principle applies to personal items." When he finished, Lukas gathered the sides of his jacket to form a bundle. As he pulled me up, his hand slipped under the edge of my T-shirt and slid across my bare skin.

"Wait. You missed one." I pointed at the triangular sliver embedded with a blue plastic eye. Black script was scrawled across the inside. "Something's written on it."

Lukas picked it up, keeping one arm firmly around me, and turned over the chipped porcelain: Millicent Avery. Middle River, Maryland.

"What do you think it means?"

"Maybe it's the name of the person who made the

doll." Lukas handed me the shard, and I slipped it in my pocket.

As he eased me down the steps, I leaned against his chest and listened to his heartbeat, focusing on the soothing rhythm instead of the vicious ache in my muscles. A sudden rush of fear swept through me.

What if the little girl isn't the only spirit in the house?

At the bottom of the stairs, the door was open and bits of gray light reflected off the dusty chandelier and glittered across the floor. It reminded me of the snow globe with the miniature version of Lilburn trapped inside something that was once beautiful.

Relief swept over me as we crossed the threshold.

Jared barreled around the side of the house before we made it down the front steps, rage coming off him in waves. Alara and Priest struggled to keep up. Lukas' arm was still around my waist, and suddenly I felt self-conscious.

Ignoring a rush of dizziness, I pulled away.

"What happened?" Jared demanded, his anger completely focused on Lukas.

"The vengeance spirit of a little girl was in there—"

"Alara said you almost got her killed," Jared shouted. It sounded like he actually cared about what happened to me.

Alara looked stunned. "That's not what I said."

Lukas' hands curled into fists at his sides. "Because she would've been safer with you? We both know putting other people first isn't your strong suit."

Jared flinched as if his brother had punched him.

Alara elbowed her way between them. She held up a silver disk with a circle of blue glass in the center. "You two can argue later. We need to find the rest of the Shift."

Jared didn't move.

Lukas dropped his jacket on the ground, revealing broken bits of the doll. "These need to be burned."

"There's writing on this one." I fished the shard out of my pocket and handed it to Priest.

"Guys?" Priest stared at the piece of porcelain in his hand.

"What if something had happened to her?" Jared demanded, his eyes still fixed on his brother. "The four of us can't do this alone."

The words hung in the air for a moment as the truth sank in. Jared didn't feel responsible for me. I was a means to an end.

I pushed past him, ignoring the pain racing up my back.

"Guys!" Priest yelled this time.

Jared spun around. "What?"

The broken piece of the doll was still in Priest's palm. "This is my granddad's handwriting."

16. A BREAK IN THE LINE

I waited for sleep to find me. But I couldn't stop thinking about the last few days and what Jared said outside of Lilburn. I knew Lukas and Jared had saved my life that first night because they were convinced I was one of them—the missing fifth member they needed.

I also knew that when I climbed into the van with them, I didn't believe it.

But I still got in. Because unlike Jared, Lukas, Alara, and Priest, I was alone. They had each other now, protected by the barrier belonging provides.

I wanted desperately to belong to something—to face the real and emotional demons of the world with someone beside me. But that was impossible. The only person I belonged to now was myself.

Climbing out of bed quietly, I wandered to the window and propped my elbows on the sill. The full moon glowed above the rooftops. It reminded me of my mom. She used to say that a moon like this was full of wishes and that if one of those wishes belonged to you it might come true when the moon broke open and the cycle began all over again. Maybe I hadn't made enough wishes.

I took one last look at the alleyway and dragged my arms off the windowsill. Carrying my boots, I tiptoed toward the break in the sheets.

I was almost at the door when I heard a voice. "Going somewhere?"

Jared was hunched over Priest's worktable under the dim glow of an emergency lantern.

Of course he's awake. He probably never sleeps.

I slipped on my boots and walked over. Priest's journal lay open to the diagram of the Shift. Jared waited for a response, his features almost ethereal in the lantern light.

"I'm leaving."

"I guessed that much. Mind if I ask why?"

"I'm not one of you." My chest tightened. "I proved that today."

"Because you couldn't take down a vengeance spirit the first time out?"

"Because I almost got myself killed. And Lukas and Alara could've been hurt."

Jared's bloodshot eyes met mine, and this time he

didn't look away. "You think you're the only one who's been attacked by a vengeance spirit?" His voice sounded deeper—more his own and less like Lukas'.

"I'm not?"

"No. And you won't be the last." He rubbed his hands over his face. "We're being hunted by a demon. The five of us need to stick together."

Five of us.

I felt the sting of the words again. "Yeah, you made that pretty clear today."

He seemed confused. "What are you talking about?"

"The only reason you care about what happens to me is because you think I'm the missing member of the Legion." I fought to keep my voice steady, but the anger burning through me seeped out with every syllable.

"Kennedy, I'm sorry if I—"

"Don't." I held up my hand. I didn't want his pity. I wanted my old life back—my mom or Elle—someone who cared about me. "Stop wasting your time and go back to looking for the right person."

He walked around the table until he was standing in front of me. "I don't think I'm wasting my time."

Everything I'd been trying so hard to hold inside came spilling out. "I'm not like the rest of you. My mom never said a word about any of this, and no one in my family ever chose me for anything."

Unless my dad choosing to leave me counts.

Jared took a step closer, staring down at me with an intensity that sent a shiver through me. "That doesn't mean you aren't the one."

How could I tell him that my own father had walked away from me without even saying good-bye?

Jared's blue eyes remained locked on mine, and it didn't feel like he was looking at me. It felt like he was looking *into* me.

I wondered what he saw.

"Maybe you want to believe it's me so you can stop searching," I said quietly.

"Are you trying to convince me or yourself?" Jared's eyes still hadn't left mine. He paused, choosing his words carefully. "The Legion is the only way to stop Andras. So before you walk away, you'd better be sure. Or a lot of innocent people are gonna die."

Now I was responsible for other people's lives? Keeping myself alive was hard enough.

I felt the weight of his words bearing down on me.

Before I could respond, shouts cut through the silence. They were coming from the opposite side of the warehouse.

Jared took off running.

On the other side of the sheet, Lukas, Priest, and Alara crowded around the window as the metal frame rattled.

Thick screws untwisted themselves and hit the concrete floor one after another.

Lukas pressed his palms against the frame, trying to hold it in place. "I don't know what happened. The window was salted, but there's a break in the line."

It was the same window I'd been looking out not even an hour ago.

A break in the line.

I lifted my arm slowly. A thin layer of white dust coated the inside of my forearm from wrist to elbow. Jared noticed and pulled me closer to get a better look. He touched the crystals and brushed them off my skin as if he expected to see something underneath.

"I didn't realize—"

Jared cut me off. "We have to leave. Now." He dropped his voice so no one else could hear him. "Don't say anything about this. I'll handle it."

Alara started to pour another salt line along the windowsill.

Jared took the bag from her and tossed it on the floor, white crystals spraying across the gray concrete. "There's no point. It won't be long before Andras finds out about this place." He turned to Lukas and Priest. "Grab the gear. We're gone."

Alara pushed past me. "Let's make sure we can get out first."

The window rattled despite the fresh salt. Maybe nothing was coming in, but something definitely wanted to. Jared fought to hold the frame in place, but only a few rusted screws remained.

I reached for the loose side of the window, but Jared nodded toward the sheets. "Help Priest. We need to take as much as we can."

I hesitated.

Another screw shot out of its casing and rolled across the floor.

I ran.

"Alara, a little help here!" Jared yelled. She slipped through the sheets carrying a stainless steel bowl. She scooped out a handful of dark green mud and smeared it over the glass, in the shape of an X.

I passed Lukas shoveling armloads of books and clothes into backpacks, but I didn't stop until I reached Priest.

Two duffel bags lay open on his worktable, and he was tossing everything from weapons to tools and scrap metal inside. I grabbed stuff from the metal shelves, but I didn't know what to take. Boxes of nails and ammunition, or tools?

"Is it another poltergeist?"

Priest shook his head, blond hair hanging in his eyes. "Don't know. Wanna stay and find out?"

Glass shattered, the sound echoing against the cinder block walls.

Jared burst through the sheets with Lukas and Alara. "We have to go."

I grabbed one of the bags and ran for the door. Priest yanked the other one off the table and the handle ripped, sending screwdrivers and ammo flying across the floor. He dropped to his knees, scooping up whatever he could carry.

Metal groaned somewhere on the opposite side of the warehouse, louder than a hundred screws hitting the floor.

Alara's eyes darted around the room. "We're not going to be able to get out."

Priest abandoned the broken bag. "Get the tank."

Jared yanked a red fire extinguisher off the wall.

"On three." He nodded at Lukas. "One, two, three."

Lukas threw open the door, and Jared bolted outside, spraying a heavy layer of white mist around us. Within seconds, we were all covered in the sticky solution.

"Get in the van." Lukas practically threw me inside.

Jared peeled away from the curb as Priest wiped the salt off his face.

"That was killer. I'll have to make more of those babies." He lifted something out of the soaked duffel. "At least I've got my torch. You never know when you'll need to set something on fire."

I hugged my knees and tried to stop shaking.

There would be no sneaking off in the middle of the night after this—not to Elle's, or my aunt's, or the stupid boarding school I'd never seen. The demon had already found me twice, and he'd find me again.

I watched as the warehouse grew smaller and smaller. In the space of a few seconds, it seemed impossibly far away.

Another safe place that wasn't safe anymore.

17. MIDDLE RIVER

We're missing a lot of gear, not to mention weapons and ammo." Priest sat across from me in the back of the van, rummaging around in his duffel bag. He looked even younger in the colored flashes of the traffic lights.

"You can make more." Lukas didn't sound very convincing.

"Not without my tools and a place to work."

Guilt twisted in my stomach. I wanted to apologize, but Jared kept stealing glances at me in the rearview mirror, silently reminding me not to say anything. Maybe there was a reason, something else I didn't understand, like the red circles on the map and the salt line.

I watched the dark streets go by, empty except for a couple of kids huddled together, smoking cigarettes under a broken liquor store sign. Their jackets were dirty and ripped, their faces worn in less definable ways. Probably runaways.

Like me.

Alara unzipped one of the backpacks that Lukas had grabbed on the way out. "I have my grandmother's notebook with her recipes for spells and wards, but it'll be hard to replace the herbs and supplies. It's not like they sell lodestones and cowrie shells at the mall."

"We can't go back." Jared sounded determined. "Priest can make more weapons, and we'll replace everything else."

She glared at him. "You mean I'll replace it."

"You're the one with the trust fund." Lukas winked at her. "But you're welcome to the twenty in my wallet."

"It's not a revolving line of credit," she said. "I only get a certain amount every month."

I remembered Alara mentioning that Lilburn reminded her of her house. I thought she was talking about the antiques or the chandeliers, not the actual mansion.

Priest shook his head, doubtful. "I can't weld just anywhere."

"Don't worry. We'll find somewhere." Jared forced a smile, but his nails were bitten down to the quick.

"Can we listen to some music or something?" I asked.

Everyone groaned.

Jared shook his head. "Don't start."

"Come on, play your favorite CD for Kennedy." Lukas smiled and turned around in the seat like he was about to reveal his darkest secret—or his brother's. "And I do mean CD."

Jared elbowed him. "Whatever. The van's old."

"So is that CD." Lukas pressed a few buttons and 1980s music blasted out of the speakers.

It sounded familiar. "Is this from a movie?"

They all burst out laughing.

Jared hit the volume control with his free hand, managing to turn it down a notch for every three Lukas turned it up.

"Make it stop," Priest whined. "My ears are bleeding."

Lukas finally gave up and let Jared shut it off, but even Alara couldn't keep a straight face. "It's the theme song from this old and totally lame movie called *The Lost Boys*."

"It's a good movie," Jared shot back, his face flushed.

Priest cleared his throat and did a bad imitation of an adult's voice that sounded a lot like my math teacher's. "I hear the soundtrack's pretty good, too, kids."

"You're lucky I can't weld." Jared tried to look annoyed, but his mouth turned up at the corners.

Priest tossed his torch on the seat next to me. His name was soldered into the metal handle.

"Is Priest your real name?" I'd been curious since the first time I heard it.

He grinned. "No. It's kind of an inside joke."

"Another joke? I'm not sure I can take it."

"This is a good one," Lukas said. "So the first time I watched him build a gun, I said it seemed like a crazy specialty for the descendant of a priest. Even an ex-priest."

Priest pulled his hood over his head. "And I said building vengeance spirit hunting weapons is a religion, and I'm the high priest. Except I can hook up with girls."

Everyone started laughing. It felt like we all stopped holding our breath at exactly the same moment, and we were regular kids again—driving home from a party to raid the fridge. Instead of wishing we still had a place to call home.

⊣ • ⊢

"You see anything?"

Priest flipped through his journal and ran the blue glass disk over the pages, hoping to decipher lines of hidden text.

I didn't, and we both knew it.

We were sitting at a booth in a diner outside of Baltimore. After two waffles and a cup of coffee spiked with cinnamon, I felt like myself again.

Lukas stirred his strawberry shake with a straw. "I think I'm going to be sick."

Alara rolled her eyes. "What did you expect? You're drinking a milk shake for breakfast."

"Want the rest?" He pushed the glass in her direction.

She eyed the glass like it was full of motor oil. "You know I don't eat pink food."

"Are you allergic to strawberries?" I asked.

"No. I just don't eat anything pink," she said, as if it was perfectly logical.

"Why not?"

Alara gave me a long look and emptied what had to be the tenth packet of sugar into her coffee. "In my family, pink symbolizes death. I would rather eat a rat."

Priest pointed at her cup. "With extra sugar."

Jared sat alone at the counter, staring out the window at the nothingness you see when you're too lost in thought to see anything else. I wondered why he was sitting alone. Why he always set himself apart from everyone else, like he was the one who didn't belong.

He caught me watching him, but instead of looking away, he held my gaze.

I walked over to the empty seat next to him. "Can I sit?"

"Be my guest." Jared's army jacket was balled up in his lap, and he was wringing it between his hands.

For a moment, neither of us spoke, the silence building a bridge between us.

"This is my fault." I needed to say it out loud.

"It isn't."

I looked out the window, my stomach twisted in knots.

I was embarrassed to face him. "You guys were safe in the warehouse until I showed up."

He leaned forward, resting his elbows on his knees. "We're never safe, not really."

"At least you had a place to sleep." I felt responsible for everything that had happened—even my mom's death. What if I had led the demon to her somehow, the same way I led the vengeance spirits to the warehouse?

Jared rubbed his eyes, and I realized how tired he looked—the kind of tired that went *way* beyond a lack of sleep. The kind that came from carrying something you couldn't put down, or share. "No one told you the windowsills were salted. I'm the one who screwed up." Jared dropped his head and leaned forward so I couldn't see his face anymore. "It's not the first time."

"Because you didn't tell me?"

"No—" He laced his fingers behind his neck like he was shielding himself from an unseen attack. "Forget it."

He reached for the coffee cup, and his T-shirt slid up, revealing a tattoo of a bird on his upper arm. It wasn't a raven or a hawk—the type I would've expected to see inked on the skin of someone like Jared. The bird looked almost delicate.

"What's that?" I pointed at the tattoo, accidentally grazing his skin. He jerked away.

I started to get up, trying to hide my embarrassment.

Jared's hand closed around my wrist, blue eyes pleading.

Heat rushed through my body like a shot of adrenaline. I froze, paralyzed by a feeling I recognized immediately. The one I felt when Chris used to hold my hand, and all I could think about was his skin against mine and the emotions churning inside me—the feeling that kept me from seeing the truth about him. Chris was scarred and damaged, and he left me with scars of my own.

I couldn't handle any more.

Jared stared at me, his hand still curled around my wrist. "It's a black dove," he said quietly. "The priests chose it because black doves are rare and small in number, like the Legion. And a dove is the only bird the devil can't transform into, which means a demon can't either."

He watched me, measuring my reaction.

I sat back down and my wrist slid from his hand. "So you believe in the devil?"

"It doesn't matter." Jared hesitated. "He believes in us."

I hoped this was another piece of information his father had passed down and not something he knew firsthand.

"Are you guys gonna help us out or what?" Priest called across the empty diner.

Lukas glanced over at us. He seemed disappointed and turned away. I felt a pang of guilt. It was hard to walk the line between the two of them, especially when it shifted constantly. One minute they were defending each other against paranormal entities, and the next they were at each other's throats.

Jared followed me back to the booth, and he slipped into silence.

Alara had turned her attention away from the offensive pink shake and back to the broken piece of the doll. "Middle River. I've seen that name somewhere before." She scanned her journal until she reached a page with a yellowed newspaper clipping taped in the corner. Above the article was a faded photo of a young woman in a floral dress, holding a little boy's hand. "I can't believe it. My grandmother told me this story a hundred times, but she never mentioned the name of the woman or where it happened."

Priest leaned over Alara's shoulder. He was the only person she seemed to allow into her personal space. "What's the deal?"

"This wealthy doctor had an affair with the seamstress who worked at his estate. Six or seven years later, the guy came home drunk and confessed everything to his wife. She went nuts and dragged the seamstress's little boy down to the well.

"The child's mother tried to stop her, but the woman pushed the kid over the side. He couldn't swim, so his mom jumped in after him. She broke her neck in the fall, and the boy drowned. According to this article, her name was Millicent Avery."

"You think one of the pieces of the Shift is hidden there?" It was the first thing Lukas had said since Jared and I sat down.

Priest slid the strawberry shake in front of him. "Alara's grandmother was the only member of the Legion my granddad knew how to contact. If he left the clue for her at Lilburn, it makes sense that it leads to a place Alara's grandmother knew about."

"Were they friends?" I asked.

Alara shook her head, dark curls falling over her shoulder. "No, the chain of information moves in one direction. Priest's grandfather knew my grandmother's name, but she didn't know his. Lukas' uncle was the only member she knew how to contact."

"Even our uncle didn't know the identity of anyone in the Legion except our father," Lukas added. "Dad's contact was the missing member. He was the only person in the Legion who would've had information about two different members—our uncle and your mom."

I mapped it out in my mind: Priest's grandfather to Alara's grandmother; her grandmother to Lukas and Jared's uncle; their uncle to their dad; their dad to the fifth member; and the fifth member to Priest's grandfather. I realized why the missing member was so important. The fifth member didn't just make the Legion stronger. That person also completed the chain of information.

I looked at Alara. "If your grandmother and Priest's granddad weren't friends, how did he know to hide the disk in Middle River?" I asked Alara.

"My grandmother owned a bakery in El Portal, where we lived in Florida. Sometimes messages showed up. They were always encrypted, in envelopes with no return address. She'd take them in the back to her real shop where she made her wards, and decipher them. Maybe he sent her the article about Millicent Avery, or told her the disk was there."

I tried to imagine living with the rules and secrets the four of them seemed so comfortable with. Jared and Lukas had each other, but what about Alara and Priest? Did they have friends back home?

Alara touched the newspaper clipping. "My grandmother told me that story so many times. She said a good mother always protects her child."

"Maybe Millicent is protecting something else now," I said.

"If a piece of the Shift is with her, you know what that means." Priest shook his head.

"It's in the well," Lukas finished.

Alara threw a napkin over the offensive pink shake. "Then we should get going."

Jared nodded at the TV mounted on the wall. "I vote for sooner," he whispered.

The volume was turned down low, but an orange news ticker ran across the bottom of the morning show feed: AMBER ALERT—KENNEDY WATERS, AGE 17. LAST SEEN AT HER HOME IN GEORGETOWN. My yearbook photo smiled back from the screen.

I strained to hear the newscaster's voice. "Kennedy Waters is seventeen years old, five foot four and one hundred twenty pounds, with long brown hair and brown eyes. She was last seen on November thirtieth at her home on O Street, in Georgetown." A shaky camera panned my street and stopped on what was left of my front yard. There were cops everywhere—red and blue lights flashed in the background.

Jared dropped the van keys in my hand and gestured at the door without a word. Then he walked up to the register and ordered a cup of coffee to distract the waitress while I slipped out.

From the front seat of the van, I watched Jared flirt with a woman old enough to be his mom, while Lukas casually gathered up the journals. Alara slipped on her black leather jacket, and Priest stuffed his gadgets and screwdrivers in his backpack.

If you didn't know any better, they looked like four regular teenagers grabbing coffee on their way to school—the guy no one knew anything about because he wouldn't let anyone get close, the kid genius who skipped three grades and still knew all the answers in Calculus, the girl who all the guys wanted to date but they were too intimidated to approach, and the sweet guy who seemed like the boy-next-door but had too many secrets to qualify. I knew they were all those things and none of them.

They were part of something bigger.

As they walked through the glass door, for the first time I imagined that I was part of it, too.

18. A GOOD MOTHER

The abandoned estate was a few miles outside of Middle River, its perimeter marked by a barbed-wire fence nailed into a row of scarred trees. A gate secured by a rusty chain blocked the dirt road leading up to the house. Whoever lived here definitely hadn't wanted any visitors.

Lukas opened the storage space in the floor of the van, and Priest grabbed a nylon rope and a pair of bolt cutters. Considering that Priest traveled with his own blowtorch, bolt cutters weren't a big surprise.

Alara was the one who used them to cut the chain. She tossed the broken links in the dirt, then leaned in and whispered something to Jared. His eyes darted in my direction.

"It's safer for everyone," Alara said, a little louder than necessary.

"What's safer for everyone?" They were obviously talking about me.

Alara crossed her arms. "I think you should wait here."

I thought about Lilburn, and the way I froze instead of running when Lukas told me to get out of the house. "I know I made some mistakes—"

"Mistakes?" Alara snapped. "You almost got us all killed last night."

My throat went dry. She knew.

Lukas turned to Alara. "What are you talking about?"

She looked right at me. "Who do you think broke the salt line?"

I wanted the ground to open up and swallow me. Anything was better than the way Alara was looking at me. I thought about Markus' journal entry, and the way one misplaced line had been the difference between controlling a demon and unleashing one. My ignorance could've cost them their lives. Despite the millions of pointless images and textbook pages my memory had recorded over the years, it hadn't helped me remember the one piece of information I'd actually needed.

"She didn't know," Jared said before I had a chance to say anything. "It was an accident."

"I should have—"

Jared cut me off. "I told her not to say anything. There was no point."

Why was he defending me?

Lukas leaned against the van, watching his brother. "You still should've told us. Secrets are dangerous." The way he said it sounded like a threat.

Jared stayed silent.

"I—I'm so sorry," I stammered.

Priest stepped between them. "We've been training for years, and Kennedy only found out about all this a few days ago. There's a learning curve."

"Look at her." Alara said it like an accusation. "She belongs at a football game with a plastic cup in her hand."

Lukas walked over and squeezed her shoulder gently. "It was an accident."

Alara shrugged him off, and they stared at each other until they seemed to arrive at a silent agreement. But she still didn't say a word as we walked toward the gate that stood between us and the hill leading up to the estate or when we stepped over the broken chain snaking through the dirt like another line I shouldn't cross.

I watched the four of them climb the hill ahead of me. How many mistakes would they forgive?

How many more would I make?

Lukas slowed his pace until I fell in step next to him. I kept my eyes trained on the ground.

"Don't worry about Alara. You'll be swapping weapons in a few days."

A smile tugged at the corners of my lips.

He dipped his head trying to get me to look at him. "Is that a smile?"

I flashed him a real one.

The crumbling stone house came into view, an empty shell left to rot in the middle of nowhere. "Creepy, huh?" he said.

"And the house with the psychotic kid and her broken doll wasn't?"

"True. But something about this place feels wrong," he said.

Alara stood at the top of the rise. "That's because people were murdered here."

The stone well waited in the distance, looking more like an illustration from a fairy tale than the scene of two vicious killings.

"I'll check it out," Jared said, but Lukas was already walking past him.

"I've got it."

Lukas crossed the dead grass, and I held my breath as he leaned over the edge of the well. He circled the well, waving an EMF detector around the chipped stones. "I've got nothing."

We crowded around the opening. The stones spiraled into the black water below. I imagined falling in and trying to grab the slick rocks to climb back up. It would be impossible, especially if you were a little boy.

"Where would your grandmother hide the disk?" Jared asked.

I swallowed hard, anticipating her answer.

"Knowing her?" Alara stared into the well. "Down there."

"Why would your families hide the pieces in such dangerous places if they knew you guys would have to find them eventually?" I asked.

"Not necessarily." Priest dropped a rock in the well and waited for it to hit the bottom. "Maybe they planned to go back for the pieces themselves. Or they were going to prepare us, but never got the chance. I doubt they all expected to die on the same day."

It made sense.

Alara unpacked her gear. "If they made it easy for us, it would be easy for Andras, too. He controls a lot of spirits."

"Okay," Jared said. "So who's going in?"

"Are you insane?" Even if you ignored the fact that two people had died in there already, the well was a death trap. It looked like it got progressively wider toward the bottom, but the mouth was barely the width of my shoulders. And there was no telling what was lurking under the water. Bones, for one thing.

"You think Priest's grandfather randomly wrote the name of this place in a doll with the disk inside?" Jared took off his jacket and tossed it on the grass.

Alara rolled her eyes. "You'll never fit in there. It's too narrow at the top."

"I'll go." Priest tied the nylon rope around his waist.

Jared yanked it loose. "Forget it."

"Why? Because I'm not as strong or fast as the rest of the superheroes?" Priest's huge headphones were still hanging around his neck, which didn't help his case.

"No one said that." Lukas reached out to put his hand on Priest's shoulder, but he jerked away.

"You don't have to." Priest's expression hardened. "How many times have I stayed behind? And when I do come, I always go with Jared so he can babysit me."

"That's because you're valuable," Lukas said. "We can't afford to lose you."

"We're all valuable. But you guys think I'm a kid who can't take care of himself." There was a hopelessness in Priest's voice that I'd never heard before.

Alara pulled her hair into a ponytail. "I'll do it."

Lukas sighed. "You're claustrophobic. You'll have a panic attack and pass out before you make it halfway down."

She leaned over the edge of the well again. "I don't

have a choice. I'm the only one besides Priest and Kennedy who can fit through the opening."

My skin went cold. I didn't want to climb in that hole—a reeking pit of dark water where two people had died.

Jared bent down to grab his jacket. "Screw it. Let's get out of here. We'll figure out something else."

"You're going to walk away without the disk instead of letting me try?" Priest's shoulders sagged.

"I'll go," I offered halfheartedly.

Alara rolled her eyes. "Nice try. You look like you're going to puke."

Lukas studied me for a second like he was considering the possibility, and Priest lost it. "Are you seriously thinking about letting her go instead of me? She just learned how to use an EMF."

"Fine." Jared tossed Priest the rope. "But you'd better do exactly what I tell you."

"I'll do exactly what you tell me, *and* what you don't." Priest took off his green and black high-tops and peeled off his hoodie before Jared could change his mind.

Lukas tied the other end of the rope around his own waist, and Jared grabbed the section between his brother and the edge of the well.

Alara handed Priest a long cold-iron rod. "After this, you need to invent a gun that works underwater."

"I'll get right on it." Priest swung his other leg over the side and slid down the moldy stones.

He was almost at the bottom when he looked up and smiled, just as a gnarled hand broke through the surface.

19. DARK WATER

The hand reached up from beneath the rancid water and grabbed Priest's leg. His eyes widened in terror as the hand jerked his body off the wall. He let out one strangled scream before the water swallowed him.

A terrifying reality hit me.

Spirits are capable of touching people.

Priest's head burst through the black surface for a second. He thrashed desperately, only to disappear again.

"We have to do something!" I shouted.

Jared threw his leg over the side and tried to force his body into the narrow opening. But his shoulders were too wide.

Alara grabbed the back of his shirt and dragged him out. "Move or I can't take a shot."

She fired liquid-salt rounds into the well, but they didn't have any effect.

Priest pushed up through the churning water again, with a bony arm locked around his throat. A woman's bruised and bloated face rose from the waves, filthy well water running down her cheeks like black tears. Her neck was broken, her head hanging unnaturally to one side.

"Get out of our well." Her raspy voice echoed against the stones.

"Millicent." Alara leaned over the edge. "I know what happened to your son. I know what they did."

Jared and Lukas struggled to pull the rope up. But even their combined weight was no match for the spirit of a mother who had witnessed her child's murder.

The spirit tightened her hold around Priest's neck. He sputtered and coughed, choking on the sloshing water.

"I won't let you take anything else from us," she hissed.

Priest was drowning in a putrid sewer of rot, and I was the only one who could help him. There was nothing to think about—not the darkness or the depth or the murderous spirit.

I wound the rope around my arm and climbed over the side.

Jared's fingers clamped down on my wrist, his blue eyes wild. "What are you doing?"

It wasn't the same fear I saw when Priest hit the water. This fear was for me.

"He's drowning. Just tell me how to stop her." Bile rose in my throat as Priest gagged and thrashed below us.

Millicent looked up at me, a milky film coating her eyes like cataracts. "They took what was mine. Now I'll take what is yours."

The spirit tightened her withered arm around Priest's neck. Her nails dug into his skin as she forced him under with her.

"Jared, you have to let me do this." I eased my hand from his grip and started sliding down the rope.

"Wait." Jared held out a long iron rod like the one Priest had taken with him. "If you stab her with this, it'll destroy her."

My hand closed over the metal, but he didn't let go.

"Don't get hurt." It was a plea, not an order.

The well grew wider about halfway down. I lowered myself into the water carefully, aware that Priest was somewhere below me. There was no way to predict the depth—until the slimy liquid rose to my chin and my feet still hadn't touched the bottom. I treaded water, reaching out blindly for Priest.

Something grabbed my waist.

Priest's head burst through the surface again. He gagged and coughed up water, his skin turning blue.

I managed to pull him toward me without going under myself. "Priest? Can you hear me?"

He only nodded.

A cold hand touched my leg and brittle hair brushed against my neck.

"I can hear you," Millicent whispered.

I thrust the rod behind me, and it slid effortlessly through the water. How would I know if I hit her? Would she feel solid?

Millicent wound my hair around her arm and yanked hard. The rod slipped out of my hand. I tried to grab it, but my head snapped back. Priest shouted something, but I couldn't hear him over Millicent's breath and the blood pounding in my ears.

Rancid liquid filled my mouth as the curtain of water closed above me. The world swayed with the ripples, shapes distorting and disappearing.

Until I ran out of air.

I fought the instinct to breathe, but it was impossible. Water filled my lungs, and the pressure hit me like a fist. Millicent slid one arm around my neck, and my body bucked against her.

Voices echoed above me.

My thoughts tripped over themselves and my vision blurred....

Without warning, the vise grip released me.

I shot up to the surface, the light getting closer and closer until I broke through.

My body convulsed, the water forcing its way back out of my lungs in violent bursts. I gasped, desperate for air.

"Kennedy?" Priest held the collar of my T-shirt, trying to keep my head above water. He shoved me behind him, and I clung to the stones, my hands slipping down the sludge-covered walls.

I coughed, the air coming in huge gulps.

A hand emerged from the water, long nails dragging across the stone.

Priest raised his arm above his head. Something gleamed in his hand, thin and sharp at one end. He drove it down into the spirit's neck.

Millicent let out a tortured wail before she exploded just like the girl in my bedroom. A spray of filthy water rained over us.

Priest wrapped the rope around my waist and pulled it tight, tethering us together. "Are you okay?"

"I think so." My throat burned, every word tearing at my vocal cords. "How did you stop her?"

"I still had one of the bolts I made for Lukas' crossbow in my pocket. It took two hits to take her down." His voice swelled with pride. "I can't believe you came after me. That was Legion all the way."

"You saved my life." I could still feel the water in my lungs, the pressure, and her arm around my neck.

He smiled. "I am the high priest, remember?"

"I'm pulling you guys up." Lukas' voice sounded shaky, or was it Jared's? I couldn't tell over the echo of the sloshing water and our ragged breathing.

"Take Kennedy," Priest said. "I need to look for the disk."

My stomach roiled at the thought of staying in the well for another second. But we had risked our lives to find the disk, and I wasn't leaving Priest down here alone.

"I'm staying."

"You're both coming up," one of them barked.

"Give us a minute." Priest ran his hands along the slippery walls. "Check between the cracks."

We worked our way around the inside of the well until my legs started to go numb from the cold. Priest even dove to the bottom a few times, but he came up empty-handed.

"Maybe it's up there around the perimeter of the well somewhere," I said.

"We'd better get out of here anyway. Your lips are turning blue." He retied the rope, leaving us only a few feet apart, and signaled to Lukas. "Okay, pull us up."

I watched Priest rise above me, moving closer to the gray sky. My body rose out of the water slowly, grime running down my arms. As my feet lifted out of the water, I felt a tiny hand close around my ankle.

It was impossible. I had watched her explode. Then I remembered.

She wasn't the only one who died in the well.

The boy's spirit looked like he was standing on top of the water, but his feet were just below the surface. The dark water splashed against his shins as if it was only inches deep.

"Wait." His voice was tiny. The boy's fingers uncurled from my skin as he reached into his pocket with his other hand. He pulled out a muddy silver disk, exactly the same size as the one we found at Lilburn.

"Lower me back down," I said.

"No way!" Lukas yelled. I could see his black jacket at the edge of the well. He tugged the rope harder.

"I'll untie myself," I threatened.

Lukas hesitated, then lowered me a few inches.

"A little more." I held out a shaking hand.

The boy dropped the disk in my palm.

"We're supposed to look after it, but I don't wanna stay here without Mamma. I'm scared of the water," he said. "Don't tell her I gave it to you."

"I won't."

The boy smiled and he faded away.

Lukas hauled me over the side and untied the frayed rope. He pulled the last end free and paused, his hand lingering on my waist. "You scared the crap out of me, you know that?"

"Sorry," I whispered.

Jared stood a few feet behind his brother, watching us. For a split second, I held his gaze, wishing I could be braver.

Not the kind of bravery it took to climb into the well,

but the kind it would take to act on what I was feeling right this second—to run over and throw my arms around Jared until everything else disappeared. But I wasn't that brave, and I didn't want to feel anything when it came to Jared. Not when I knew how easily a guy like him could hurt me.

Lukas wiped the dirt off my face with the edge of his T-shirt. He made me feel safe in a world I didn't understand, while Jared always left me feeling off balance. Like the way he was making me feel right now.

Heat spread across my cheeks.

I wondered if Lukas noticed—if he thought it was because of him.

Priest rushed over to Jared. "Did you see me take out that vengeance spirit? Don't tell me it wasn't badass."

Jared looked away, breaking the connection between us, and gave Priest a weak smile. "Yeah, it was badass all right. And dumbass."

"Whatever." Priest stripped off his shirt and yanked on his dry hoodie, flipping up the hood.

"Here." I handed Priest the disk.

"That's what I'm talking about." He grinned and examined it. "Based on the diagram and the size of the disks, the cylinder should be about the size of a coffee can."

Alara touched my arm gently. "Are you okay?"

For a second, I was speechless. It was something a friend would do, not the girl who couldn't stand me.

I rubbed my neck, trying to get rid of the feeling of

163

Millicent's arm wrapped around it. "I didn't know spirits could touch us like that. She felt so real."

"Not all of them can, but she was a full body apparition. Some of them feel as real as you and me."

"How can you tell the difference?"

Alara stepped behind me, helping me wring the disgusting water out of my hair. "Sometimes you can't."

"Damn." Priest winced, shaking his wrist in the air. "I must have cut myself."

It was worse than that.

When he pulled up his sleeve, lines were carving themselves into the underside of his wrist like they were being guided by an invisible blade. Deep bloodless indentations remained etched in his flesh.

I gasped. "Oh my god."

Jared squeezed Priest's shoulder. "You're getting your mark."

What was he talking about? And why was he so calm while something sliced into Priest's skin?

I pointed at the lines. "Does someone want to explain that?"

"When the original members of the Legion summoned Andras, they carved part of his seal into their flesh to bind him," Lukas said. "It was supposed to help them control the demon. When a member of the Legion dies, their part of the seal transfers to the person chosen to replace them."

"Why wasn't it there before?"

"You have to earn it by destroying a paranormal entity." Priest stared down at the mark in awe.

Alara twisted her eyebrow ring, pouting. "I still don't have one."

Lukas nudged her. "You will. Maybe you can take down a pink milk shake."

"Eventually our marks will form the seal," Priest said.

"How?"

Jared pulled up his sleeve and Lukas did the same. The skin on the insides of their wrists was smooth and unmarked. Priest held out his wrist, too. Where there had been deep depressions a moment ago, the skin had completely healed.

I grabbed his wrist. "Where did the cuts go?"

"Wait." Jared nodded at Alara.

She scooped a handful of salt out of her pocket. The guys offered her their wrists and she rubbed them with the crystals. Within seconds, the indentations appeared in their skin, the lines blackening like they were filled with ink.

How is that possible?

I examined the shapes etched into their skin. None of the designs resembled the demon's seal until they bent their wrists, Lukas and Jared lining up theirs side by side, and Priest pressing the heel of his hand against Jared's. It created an *L* shape that transformed into three-fifths of the seal. After a minute, the lines faded again.

"So you don't have one?" I asked Alara.

She brushed the salt off her hands. "Not yet. My grandmother was overprotective. But I'm not going to be the last person to get one."

"I don't think you have to worry about that." I had almost gotten myself killed again today. I obviously wasn't ready to destroy a vengeance spirit.

"You still don't believe you're one of us?" Priest asked, shaking the water out of his hair. He saved my life. This fifteen-year-old kid that I barely knew.

I looked back at Priest and gave him the only answer I could. "I don't know what I believe."

20. A SLIVER OF LIGHT

Priest wiped off the disk, revealing the red glass in the center of the silver ring. I sat on the ground wearing Lukas' jacket over my wet clothes. This time I was too cold to let my pride get in the way when he had offered.

"We should go back to the van or you guys are going to freeze to death." Two near-drownings had transformed Alara from hard-core to maternal.

"No way. The clue to finding the next piece has to be out here," Priest said.

"Where? In there?" Jared stopped pacing and gestured at the well.

"You think?" Priest raised his eyebrows.

Alara shoved him affectionately. "Don't even joke about it."

Lukas peered over the edge of the well. "No one's going back down."

"Maybe it's in the house," I offered.

"At Lilburn, the disk and the clue about this place were together." Priest sounded skeptical. "The house is pretty far away." He rolled the circle of glass between his fingers, fascinated. "Whoever designed the Shift must've been a genius."

As he rotated the disk, a slash of light appeared on the side of the well.

"Did you see that?" I pointed at the spot on the gray stones.

Priest looked around. "What?"

"I saw it." Lukas gestured at the disk in Priest's hand. "Turn it again."

Priest rolled the glass one more time. The light caught in exactly the same spot as before, appearing almost fluorescent. He bent down and ran the disk along the stones, and letters appeared like they were written in glow-in-the-dark marker. "No way."

DYBBUK BOX, SUNSHINE

"What's a *dybbuk* box?" I asked.

Alara shook her head. "Don't ask."

"Wait. I know this." Lukas paced in front of the well. "My dad told me a story about one."

"So what is it?" Priest asked.

"Dad said that in Jewish folklore they believe that if you commit horrible sins when you're alive, your spirit won't be able to rest after you die," Lukas explained. "They call the disembodied spirit a dybbuk, and it wants one thing—a body to possess. My dad talked about them a few times. It always seemed random."

"You said he told you a story?" Alara asked.

Lukas nodded. "This woman came over from Poland after World War II, and the only thing she brought with her was this wine cabinet. She kept it in her sewing room and called it dybbuk. The woman never let anyone inside that room, and she left instructions for the cabinet to be buried with her when she died. But get this. The rabbi wouldn't do it. So they sold it at an estate sale."

Jared looked surprised. "I don't remember this story."

"I guess Dad didn't tell you everything." It was an obvious dig. When Jared didn't react, Lukas continued. "Anyway, this guy bought the cabinet and gave it to someone in his family as a gift. But after a few days they gave it back. He kept giving it to different family members, and every time, the person brought it back. Eventually, he got everyone together to find out what was going on. They all had similar experiences when the cabinet was in their houses—it wouldn't stay closed, it smelled like urine, and while it was in the house, they had nightmares about being beaten by an old woman and woke up covered in bruises."

"Are you making this up?" Priest brushed his damp hair out of his eyes. At least I wasn't the only one who thought it sounded completely crazy.

"He's not," Alara said. "I've heard the story, too."

"That's not even the weirdest part." Lukas paused. "All of them saw a figure moving around the house while they had the cabinet."

A chill crept up my back. Listening to the story while Lukas paced in front of the well we had almost drowned in made it more disturbing.

"What happened to it?" I asked.

Lukas shrugged. "The guy sold it. That's all I know."

Alara walked over and ran the red glass across the stones again. "Do you think this is the same box?" She sounded almost excited.

"I don't know," Lukas said. "It could be another one. But it looks like we're dealing with a dybbuk either way." The idea that there was more than one possessed box floating around the world wasn't comforting.

Jared studied the fluorescent print on the well. "What about *Sunshine*? Think it's someone's last name?"

"No." For once, I was the one with the answer. "It's a city not far from here." I drove to the art supply store there every few months to stock up on paint sticks in this amazing shade of cadmium red.

Priest slipped the disk in the pocket of his wet jeans.

We trudged back to the van scraped, bruised, and bloody—
ready to hunt down a spirit residing somewhere in its own
little piece of Sunshine.

⇥ • ⇤

Everyone was exhausted, and no one wanted to sleep in
the van. My muscles were shredded and sore from tread-
ing water, and my chest ached with every breath. Priest
didn't look much better. Even the music blaring from his
headphones could barely keep him awake.

"If we're staying in a hotel, I need to find an ATM."
Alara sat in the passenger seat next to Jared. "We're low
on cash."

"I don't have any money," I whispered to Lukas.

"It's okay," Lukas said. "Alara gets money every month."

Jared pulled over in front of a bank, and she
jumped out.

I watched her walk up to the machine in her cargo
pants and combat boots. "A trust fund? Seriously?"

Priest grinned. "Never judge a girl by her piercings."

Jared scanned through the radio stations, and I heard
a familiar song.

"Wait—"

"Leave it there," Lukas said at the same time.

"Just lookin' for shelter from the cold and the pain
Someone to cover, safe from the rain...."

I stared at Lukas, shocked. "You know this song?"

It wasn't one of the Foo Fighters' most popular songs. "Home" was quiet and understated, a whisper in a world full of screams.

Lukas gave me a sheepish smile. "It's my favorite."

Warmth spread across my cheeks, and suddenly it felt like we were sharing something intimate in front of a room full of people. I was drawn to the song the first time I heard it, right after my mom died. I must have played it a hundred times. It became a sort of anthem, a silent prayer.

What did Lukas think about when he heard it? Did he ever sit in the car listening to it over and over? I wanted to ask him.

He looked back at me as if he wanted to ask me something, too.

Alara opened the door, breaking the thread between us.

"Are we good?" Jared asked.

"No." She sounded stunned.

"What's wrong?"

She didn't answer right away. "There's only three thousand dollars left."

Only three thousand dollars?

Jared shrugged. "You'll have more in a few weeks, right?"

Alara shook her head. "You don't get it. Someone took

money *out* of my account. Unless it was hacked, my parents are the only ones who have that kind of access."

Priest slipped off his headphones. "What are you saying?"

"It's a message." Alara got out and hit speed dial on her phone. "I need to make a call."

She paced in front of the van and, judging from her scowl, the conversation wasn't going well. The way Alara held the phone right in front of her while she shouted into it reminded me of Elle, who did almost exactly the same thing whenever one of her boyfriends screwed up. I wished she were here now.

I tried to imagine Alara and Elle meeting—two iron wills clashing, or forging into one unstoppable and sarcastic force.

Lukas watched as she screamed at the phone. "Not good."

Alara got in and slammed the door, seething. "My parents want me to come home. They've been pressuring me ever since my grandmother died. My mom thinks I don't have enough training." She laughed. "Like I'll be able to get any there. Neither one of them is part of the Legion. What do they think they're going to teach me?"

Jared seemed surprised. "You never said anything."

She reached over and turned the key in the ignition. "That's because I'm not going back."

We pulled into a motel parking lot, with a cracked vacancy sign flashing above the office. Empty beer cans littered the walkway.

"It's only for one night. How bad can it be?" Priest asked.

From Alara's perspective, it couldn't have been worse. Every door facing the lot was Pepto-Bismol pink.

She crossed her arms, defiant. "I'm not sleeping in a room with a pink door. That's where I draw the line."

Lukas got out and walked toward the office. "You can always sleep in the van."

By the time he came back with the key, Priest had persuaded Alara to check out the room. But when Lukas unlocked the door, he stopped short.

"Alara, you might want to rethink that line."

Inside, the tiny room was painted the same sickening shade of pink.

"No way." She backed up, shaking her head. "I'd rather sleep on the thirteenth floor."

Priest coaxed her across the threshold. "Don't worry. I'll protect you from the dangerous color."

The room was practically empty—two double beds with mismatched bedspreads, a broken TV on a rolling cart, and a plastic trash can that hadn't been emptied lately. Not even a cheap landscape on the tragically bare walls.

Alara crinkled her nose. "This is disgusting."

Priest fell back onto the tacky Western bedspread. "It has beds. That's all that matters."

"Two." Alara tipped her chin toward me. "And we get one of them."

"I call half of this one," Priest said. "I did almost drown."

"You're going to milk that for all it's worth, aren't you?" Alara teased.

"Ah...that would be a yes."

"You should call the first shower while you're at it," she said. "You smell even worse than Kennedy."

Jared and Lukas stood next to each other by the door. I wasn't used to seeing them side by side, with their identical broad shoulders and full lips, sleepy eyes and long eyelashes. They looked like the same person, but they were so different.

After Priest took a shower, I was voted the second dirtiest. I didn't argue. Dried well water coated my skin, and my clothes were even worse.

"Hey." Lukas stood behind me with something balled up in his hand. "I have an extra T-shirt if you need one." I hadn't thought about what I was going to put on after my shower.

"Thanks."

My scraped skin brushed his rope-burned palm. Even bloody and raw, his touch was gentle—like him. I could imagine Lukas listening to "Home," the song we both loved, whispering the lyrics to himself the way I did when I felt lost.

I closed the door and leaned against it, letting the room fill with steam. I didn't want to look at my tangled hair and grime-streaked face in the mirror. But I didn't need to see the fresh cuts on the rest of my body to know they were there. Hot water stung them as I sat on the shower floor, waiting for the brown water running off my legs to turn clear again.

The memory of Millicent's cold arm around my neck and the well water filling my lungs finally drove me out of the shower.

I slipped into Lukas' T-shirt, relieved when it grazed my knees. I was even more relieved that I had ignored Elle when she tried to convince me to trade my boy shorts for "cute" underwear, with stupid words like *pink* written on the back.

When I finally opened the door, it still felt like everyone could see right through the shirt.

Priest put on his headphones. "Anyone care if I turn off the lights?"

Thank god.

I made a beeline for the bed, tugging at the bottom of the T-shirt. A streak of blood smeared across the cotton. Between skidding across the front walk at my house and fighting off Millicent's spirit, the cuts on my hand were bleeding again. As I turned back toward the bathroom to grab a towel, Lukas stepped inside and closed the door.

Exhaustion hit as I sat on the edge of the bed waiting for him to finish. My eyes felt heavy, and I fought to stay awake.

When the door hinges creaked, I jumped. I wandered to the bathroom half asleep.

Lukas walked out barefoot and shirtless, wearing nothing but a pair of jeans. He rubbed a towel over his hair, sending streaks of water down his chest.

With nowhere else to look, I studied a bare patch on the stained carpet. "I need to grab a towel for my hand."

"Let me see." He stepped closer and took my wrist gently, his jeans brushing against my leg.

"It's no big deal." I tried to ignore the fact that I was standing in front of a beautiful boy, wearing his T-shirt.

"As long as you're all right." Lukas' hand slid from my wrist as I stepped into the harsh light of the tiny bathroom.

I rinsed my hand and knotted a hand towel around it.

When I came back out, Jared was standing there, wringing a clean shirt in his hands. I couldn't stop thinking about the way Lukas had looked without his shirt—imagining Jared that way now.

My heart hammered against my ribs. I searched for the bare spot on the carpet again, terrified he'd know exactly what I was thinking if he saw my face.

He stepped aside and gave me enough room to pass.

"I'm glad you're okay," he said softly as he shut the door.

Standing in the dark, the air still carrying the weight of the unnamed thing between us.

I fell onto the bed next to Alara and listened to the running water echoing from the shower.

Don't think about it.

Alara nudged me. "Kennedy?"

"Yeah?"

"Thanks for going after Priest back there. It took guts."

The compliment caught me off guard. "Anyone would have done the same thing."

"Not unless you're one of us." There was something about the way she said it that made it seem possible.

"Is it hard to be part of the Legion?"

Alara was quiet for a moment. "You have to give up a lot."

"Like school and your friends—"

"Like my family."

It wasn't the response I had expected. "I thought you grew up with your grandmother."

"I moved in with her when I was ten. Before that I lived with my parents and my younger brother and sister, in Miami."

"Why did you move in with her?" I was prying, but I sensed that she wanted to talk. And I missed the nights Elle and I stayed up late sharing secrets.

"My parents knew one of us would be chosen to join the

Legion before we were old enough to walk, and they knew it would be me or my sister, Maya. My grandmother wanted to pass her specialty on to a girl." Alara stared at the ceiling.

"And she chose you?"

"Not exactly. She wanted to take one of us while we were young enough for our training to become second nature, but my parents kept stalling. Eventually, my grandmother forced them to pick a date. When the day finally arrived, we knew my grandmother was coming and that one of us would be leaving with her. Maya and I sat on this green velvet sofa in the foyer, holding hands. My mother had dressed us up in these stupid taffeta dresses like we were going to a party. My parents were in my father's office with my grandmother, deciding who she was going to take. When they came back out, my mom was crying. My grandmother told her to choose."

Alara swallowed hard. "But there was no choice. Maya was fragile. She never could've handled my grandmother or the Legion. It would have destroyed her. So I lied and told them I wanted to go. I practically begged."

I tried to imagine the situation. Waiting to see if I would have to leave my mom. Volunteering to be the one. "Your parents must have missed you so much."

"They gave me away like a puppy. Now my father thinks he can just tell me to quit and summon me home like what I'm doing isn't important?"

I thought about my dad standing next to his car, staring

at me through the kitchen window. Knowing he was never coming back. Did he see how confused I looked when he drove away? Did he care?

Being given away didn't seem that different from being left behind. I understood how it felt to be broken when everyone around you was whole.

"I'm sorry."

Alara took a deep breath. "I'm not. My sister wasn't cut out for this. I am."

"What you did for her was still really brave."

"Climbing into that well was brave, too." She handed me something balled up in her fist. "Take this. You need it more than I do."

I could barely make out the object in my palm, until it caught the light from the buzzing fluorescent motel sign outside. It was the round silver medal Alara always wore around her neck. Up close, I could see the symbols etched into the surface, with what looked like a pitchfork pointing away from the center of the pendant.

"It's called the Hand of Eshu. It protects the person wearing it from evil. Maybe it will keep you from getting yourself killed."

"Thanks." I knotted the cord around my neck, wishing I could think of something more meaningful to say.

Within minutes she was asleep.

I stared into the darkness. A sliver of light crept from underneath the bathroom door. I thought about all the ways Jared could hurt me.

How much pain could I withstand before I finally broke?

21. SUNSHINE

In the morning, we stopped at 7-Eleven for coffee and batteries. Alara gave each of us five dollars in an attempt to ration our funds. Priest headed straight for the candy aisle and cleaned out the stock of watermelon sours. He had moved on to chips by the time I made it over there.

Candy wasn't really my thing. But when I was little, my dad used to bring chocolate bars home from work.

He fished the candy bar out of his jacket pocket. It had a red wrapper with 100 GRAND *printed in white block letters across the front.*

I wanted to open it, but I knew better. "I'm not supposed to eat candy before dinner."

"Today is upside-down day. That means you can have dessert first." My dad opened the wrapper and handed me one of the two pieces inside. We bit into our halves at the same time.

The red wrapper was permanently stamped in my mind, like so many other images I couldn't erase. I wanted one of those stupid candy bars more than anything right now.

I was still deciding if a stomach full of chocolate was a good idea at nine in the morning, when I noticed the guy behind the register staring. His eyes darted from the small TV on the counter and back to me, as my black and white yearbook photo flashed across the screen.

Jared walked down the aisle toward me, his back to the cashier. I didn't move, my eyes fixed on the racks.

Please don't say anything.

Another step and Jared's body blocked the guy's view.

"The guy behind the counter recognized me. Keep walking," I whispered, careful not to turn in Jared's direction. "I'll meet you behind the school we passed on the way here."

The cashier didn't take his eyes off me.

Jared walked by and stopped in front of the coffee machine at the end of the aisle, where Lukas and Priest were filling up Styrofoam cups. Jared said something, and they all laughed and elbowed each other. When Alara heard Jared laughing, she snapped to attention and zeroed in on him like he had flashed the Bat Signal.

The cashier picked up the phone.

Lukas shoved his brother and the cups slipped out of their hands, coffee splattering onto the floor.

"What are you doing back there?" The guy was off his stool and halfway down the aisle, the phone receiver still lying on the counter.

"I'm really sorry." Lukas grabbed a bunch of napkins from a nearby dispenser. "We'll clean it up."

"And you're gonna pay for those," I heard him say as the door closed behind me.

I ducked behind the 7-Eleven and followed the main road back to the elementary school, careful to stay off the shoulder in case the cashier decided to call the police. Behind the school, I huddled on a bench listening for sirens.

If the cashier did call, would the police tell my aunt I was okay?

Even though I didn't like her, she had offered to take me in after my mom died, and I owed her something for that—at least a message to let her know I wasn't lying in a ditch. I had considered calling more than once, but if the police believed someone had kidnapped me, her phone would definitely be tapped.

A disposable cell phone might throw off the police, but

I wasn't sure about a demon. That thought had stopped me from calling Elle again. Vengeance spirits had already followed me to the warehouse, and I wasn't willing to make any more mistakes.

The sirens never came, just boots crunching across the dry leaves. "Kennedy?"

"Over here."

Jared scanned the playground until he saw me, and his tense expression broke into a rare smile. "That was way too close."

"No argument here." I glanced behind him. "Where is everyone?"

"In the van. I thought four of us wandering around might look suspicious." He sat down on the other end of the bench. "How did you know that guy in the store recognized you?"

"He was watching TV, and I saw my picture on the screen."

Jared leaned forward, resting his elbows on his knees, and looked back at me. I wanted to reach out and touch the scar above his eye—to ask him how he got it.

"Maybe you should stay in the van next time," he said. "I don't know if I can pull off another performance like that."

"You were pretty convincing. I think you missed your calling."

His smile faded and silence stretched between us.

"I'm sorry," he said finally.

"For what?"

"I know you probably wish you weren't part of this." He sounded so lonely. I fought the urge to put my arms around him and breathe in the smell of salt and copper that clung to Jared even when he was only bleeding on the inside.

I wanted to tell him how lonely I was—how badly I needed someone. I wanted to tell him that and so much more. But I couldn't find the words, or I wouldn't let myself.

"That's not true."

Jared bit his lip. "Come on. You had a life—school, friends, probably a boyfriend—something better than this."

Was that really what he thought? That I walked away from the perfect life?

"If I had a boyfriend, I would've called him by now. I don't abandon the people I care about."

"I didn't mean—"

"And if by better, you mean losing my mom and packing up my whole life to move to a boarding school I'd never seen…" My voice wavered. "Then, yeah, I guess it was better."

Jared's face softened, opening up in a way that was beautiful and scary at the same time. He slid his hand slowly across the bench to the place where mine rested between us. My breath caught as he laced our fingers together.

Jared squeezed my hand and my heart jumped. "Kennedy, I wish—"

The chain-link fence rattled on the other side of the yard as Lukas hopped over it.

I pulled my hand away, leaving Jared's on the bench. But I could still feel it as if I had never let go.

⇥ • ⇤

Sunshine didn't live up to its name. The guys went into town to see what they could find out. Alara and I stayed behind and pored over the journals, searching for any information related to dybbuk boxes.

She turned to a page in hers with an elaborate symbol drawn on it—a circle with a heptagram in the center. Words in an unfamiliar language were written inside and around the circumference. It was the same symbol someone had drawn on the floor of the warehouse.

"What's that?"

"The Grand Pentacle from *The Goetia*, one of the oldest grimoires in existence. We call it the Devil's Trap. If a demon steps inside one of these, it can't get out." Alara traced the outer circle with her finger. "If the lines are precise enough, the trap can even destroy the demon."

Below it was another symbol—two perpendicular lines with an S shape above it.

Miray la was written next to it.

"Is that French?"

"Haitian Creole. It means 'the Wall.'"

"Is it like the Devil's Trap?" I asked.

She shook her head. "The Wall is just a binding symbol. It can keep a spirit bound inside, but it's not strong enough to destroy one. You have to do that yourself."

I stared at the Devil's Trap and wondered if my mom had ever seen one, trying to reconcile the woman who baked me brownies whenever I had a rough day with the missing member of the Legion.

Alara closed the book. "There's nothing in here. Hopefully, the guys are having better luck." In this situation, it was a relative term. "But you're going to need more than luck."

"What do you mean?"

She climbed into the van and came back with a duct-taped gun and a handful of liquid salt rounds. "Most people only need to know how to defend themselves against the living. I'm going to make sure you can say the same about the dead."

Alara had lent me some of her extra clothes before we left the motel, since mine smelled like sewage. Now the pockets were filled with salt rounds and cold-iron nails.

"Move your hand higher on the grip." Alara took the gun and demonstrated. "It gives you more control."

"Okay," I said, as she handed the gun back to me. I repositioned my hands and took a deep breath. I squeezed the trigger, and the salt round exploded against the ground a few feet from the tree I'd tried to hit.

Alara sighed. "Next time, try keeping your eyes open."

After an hour, I started to get the hang of it and managed to hit more than a few defenseless trees and one traumatized squirrel.

I was sitting in the grass, rubbing my boots with a rag, when Priest came around the corner wearing a bright orange hoodie with CINDY'S DINER across the front. "Did you miss me?"

Lukas and Jared were behind him, carrying two Styrofoam cups and a pink cardboard box.

I gestured at Priest's hoodie. "Subtle."

"It was this or NASCAR. And I'm not the one with my face in the newspaper."

"It was TV, not the paper," I said, like the distinction somehow affected my fugitive status.

"Not anymore." Lukas tossed me a copy of the local paper. It was open to the page with a tiny picture of me and the details of my supposed abduction.

Priest sat down next to me. "Don't worry, you're on the same page as a story about a ninety-six-year-old woman who won the lottery playing her cat's birthday. People probably won't even see it."

"And we come bearing gifts." Lukas handed us each a cup and Jared opened the box. Coffee and doughnuts, they smelled like heaven.

"That box better be the only thing that's pink." Alara ripped open several packets of sugar at once and dumped them in her cup.

I walked around to the back of the van and tossed the guns into one of the duffel bags.

"Hey." Lukas was standing behind me. "I didn't mean to sneak up on you. I just wanted to give you this." He reached under his jacket and pulled out a pad of white paper. "I know you don't have a journal from your mom, but I thought maybe you could start one. Or you can just draw in it. Priest says you're really good."

I reached for the pad and our hands touched.

There was something between us, even if it wasn't the magnetic pull I felt with Jared. I ignored the hypnotic blue eyes and soft lips they shared, and really looked at Lukas. I thought about the way I felt safe whenever he was close, and the friendship he offered as easily as a smile.

"It was all they had at 7-Eleven, but I'll get you a real one when I have a chance."

"No, it's perfect." I held it against my chest. "I miss drawing." I reached up and hugged him. "Thanks."

Lukas slid his hands around my waist and pulled me closer, and I breathed in the scent of his skin—the smell of the woods after it rained. His cheek brushed mine. "Anytime."

I slipped the pad into the duffel and followed him back to the other side of the van. Jared didn't look in our direction, his eyes glued to the ground.

"Did you guys find out anything or what?" Alara dumped two more packets of sugar into her coffee.

"Get this." Priest tore a glazed doughnut in half and shoved it in his mouth. "There's an old magic shop in town. Some weird guy owned it. The waitress at the diner said he was always traveling and bringing back all kinds of bizarre junk for his store."

Alara scrunched up her nose. "I hate magicians. They're just a step above mimes and clowns."

Priest finished off the other half of the doughnut. "You're not the only one. They found the shop owner dead in the store two weeks ago. When we asked how he died, she just kept saying it was too horrible to talk about."

"That's helpful." Alara took a doughnut out of the box, careful not to touch the pink cardboard. "Did the waitress mention a box?"

Priest shook his head. "No. But she did say it took a while before his body was discovered."

She perked up. "That's weird."

"Not really," Lukas said. "No one ever went in the store because the place smelled like cat piss."

"It could be a coincidence," I said.

Jared tossed an untouched doughnut back in the box. "He didn't have any cats."

22. THE BOX

Yellow police tape ran across the door, where a plastic sign was flipped to CLOSED. A thick layer of dust coated the shop windows, which displayed a collection of unmagical-looking items: cheap black top hats and polyester capes, a corroded birdcage with a fake dove inside, silver linking rings, and a wooden ventriloquist's dummy.

Breaking and entering in the middle of the day was risky, but every choice we made now felt like a risk. Jared parked in the back alley, hoping no one would see us, while Priest picked the lock with a piece of wire rigged specifically for the purpose.

The door swung open, and the nauseating stench of ammonia hit us.

Alara gagged. "You've gotta be kidding. I'm not going in there without a gas mask."

"Your call." Jared walked inside. The dusty haze of daylight followed him, revealing dozens of overflowing boxes, crates, and metal storage shelves.

Priest flipped a switch and fluorescent lights above us illuminated an enormous storage room filled with even more junk. "This guy was a total hoarder."

The whole place felt like the inside of Pandora's box, something best left undisturbed.

I touched the handle of the nail gun tucked in the back of my jeans for reassurance. "This doesn't seem like the kind of guy who'd have a wine cabinet."

Lukas tipped over a trash can full of dismembered doll parts, tiny flesh-colored arms and legs sticking out of the top. "It can be any kind of box."

"Someone get a reading. I can't stand this much longer," Alara mumbled, her nose buried in the crook of her arm. It hadn't taken her long to reconsider her position on urine-infested magic shops.

I reached for an EMF and my elbow hit something hard.

A huge vanishing cabinet with a crimson door loomed behind me. Inside, a painting of a snake twisted around bits of broken mirror and colored glass glued along the walls, its mouth open and ready to strike.

"Guys... this is a lot bigger than a wine cabinet."

Priest and Jared walked toward me, Priest's eyes glued to his EMF. "Hopefully, whatever's living in there isn't. The needle's going crazy."

Jared's eyes locked on mine, and my heart sped up. Until his expression changed, and I realized he wasn't looking at me anymore.

He was looking behind me.

"Kennedy, move!" he shouted.

A rush of cold air burst from the box and knocked me over. It swept past me and stopped in front of Alara. It was the torso of a man with bare milk-white skin marred by black bruises. But this thing wasn't a man. Its head was shaved and the vertebrae in its spinal column strained beneath the skin as if it was a size too small.

But where the bones ended, so did the human form— and its waist disappeared into a thick blur of white smoke.

I forced my legs to move, stumbling over the clutter.

The dybbuk whipped around, following the sound. I pressed my hand against my mouth, stifling a scream as I stared into the blackened recesses where its eyes should've been.

It reached for Alara. Her body rose off the floor as if the dybbuk was using some kind of telekinetic power. She screamed, and the force slammed her against the wall. Alara's head hit the concrete, and she slid to the floor without a sound.

Jared ran toward her. The dybbuk ripped him off his

feet, using the same supernatural power it had used to lift Alara, and hurled Jared into the metal shelves.

"Screw this." Lukas aimed and fired round after round of liquid salt. The bullets passed right through the dybbuk's pale torso and dropped to the floor on the other side.

I scrambled around the edge of the room toward Alara. She had managed to sit up, but she was still disoriented when I reached her.

"Are you okay?"

"It's so strong." Panic clung to her voice—the fearless girl I found so intimidating suddenly replaced by one as vulnerable as the rest of us.

Lukas and Priest knelt next to Jared, who lay on the floor amid a sea of severed doll limbs.

He's not moving.

There was only one way to help him. "Alara, how do we stop it?"

She stared at me blankly.

I grabbed her shoulders. "How do we destroy it?"

The dybbuk laughed, and the menacing sound echoed through the room.

It focused on Lukas and Priest, and their bodies rose in the air simultaneously. They hovered above the floor for a moment before their backs smacked against the wall, halfway between the floor and the ceiling. Their bodies slid up the wall, their shoulders and elbows cracking against the corners of the metal shelves.

"Alara, tell me what to do," I pleaded.

Her eyes darted from the dybbuk and back to me. "We have to bind that thing inside the cabinet and burn it."

"How?"

Alara blinked hard. "A binding symbol."

"Like the one from your journal?" I remembered it perfectly.

She nodded. "The Wall is the easiest. But I can't draw it without my journal, and it won't bind that thing unless the symbol looks exactly the same."

Boxes crashed to the floor as Lukas dropped onto the concrete not far from where his brother's body lay, unconscious. Lukas struggled to sit up, but he looked unsteady.

"Screw you." Priest thrashed wildly, still pinned halfway up the wall.

The dybbuk threw its pale head back and demonic laughter filled the air like a thousand pins pricking my skin.

"I can do it," I said automatically. "I remember what it looks like."

Alara shook her head. "If you make a mistake—"

The symbol formed in my mind as clearly as if I was still staring at the page. "I have a photographic memory. I won't make a mistake."

"You're serious?"

"Completely."

Alara slid the black marker out of her tool belt and

handed it to me. "I'm going to distract it, but you'll have to work fast. Then I'll find a way to lure it into the box."

The dybbuk let Priest fall and jerked his body back and forth across the floor like a rag doll without so much as a touch.

I ran for the cabinet.

I stepped inside and my eyes burned from the stench of ammonia. The snake's open mouth was only inches away from me, shards of mirror forming perfect fangs. And something else—two round pieces of green glass edged in silver stared back from the centers of its eyes.

Tiny splinters pushed their way underneath my nails as I worked one free. In the dim light, it looked exactly like the disk from inside the doll. Unfortunately, so did the other one. I slipped them both in my pocket and glanced behind me.

Alara opened the plastic bottle of holy water holstered on her belt, and dumped it over her head.

This was her plan?

I closed the cabinet door, pitching myself into darkness. Within seconds, panic set in and it felt like I was five years old again, hiding in the tiny crawl space in my mother's closet. Waiting for her to come back.

I can't stay in here.

My pulse thundered in my ears, but another sound was louder—a crash.

Was it Priest this time? Or Lukas or Alara? I pictured

Jared lying on the floor, and my heart ached. What if he needed a doctor?

What if...

A tiny crack between the hinges threw a slice of light across my boots, but there wasn't enough room for me to bend down and draw the symbol on the floor. I was going to have to do it on the ceiling, which meant sketching blind.

How would I know if I made a mistake?

"Priest? Lukas? You okay?" Alara shouted, her voice muffled by the layer of wood between us.

"Yeah."

"Get Jared out of here," she said.

"We're not leaving you guys." Lukas sounded as determined as she did.

"If you want to save your brother, you will," Alara shot back.

"Pretty girl with an ugly soul." The voice that answered this time didn't belong to Lukas. It was distorted and wrong—the sound of something horrific trying on human skin.

Working quickly, I let my mind guide the marker. I drew the first line, positioning my other hand so I'd know where to begin the horizontal line I needed to make next.

The heavy metal door to the alley slammed shut.

Someone had made it out—maybe all three of them.

But if the door was closed, the guys were locked out. I was the only one who could help Alara.

I concentrated on the one thing I had always been able to do—the skill that felt more like a curse than a gift.

My hand finally stopped when the marker finished the last line. I peeked through the crack just as the dybbuk charged Alara. When its body touched her wet skin, a hiss of white steam rose above them, and the dybbuk lurched back. I had to get that thing away from her and into the cabinet. Fast.

I flung open the door. "Hey, over here! I'm in your nasty box."

It whirled around, the blackened eye sockets facing me. "Get outtt!"

"Kennedy, no!" Alara shouted.

It was coming right at me—

Don't move until it steps inside.

I pressed my hand against the false back of the cabinet, but I wasn't quick enough.

The impact punched the air out of my lungs. A sickening sensation gripped me, like something was crawling through my body and fighting its way out the other side. I felt the dybbuk twisting and writhing like hundreds of snakes trapped under my flesh.

I threw my weight against the back of the box, and the wall sprang open.

My cheek hit the concrete and I clawed at the floor,

dragging myself away from the box. I rolled over and realized it didn't matter.

The dybbuk was trapped, its limbs jerking back each time it tried to reach outside the boundaries of the box. "What have you done, ugly soul?"

Alara ran toward me, her long legs vaulting over upended stage props that paled in the presence of real magic. She dug through her pockets and pulled out a disposable lighter, holding it against the rotted wood. The flame fluttered, then caught and climbed up the edge of the box.

"We have to get out of here," she said, shoving me toward the door.

Ash flaked in the air like peeled skin as the side of the cabinet burned, and the fire leapt from the box to the wall behind it.

"Go." Alara pushed me ahead of her.

The alley door was only a few feet away when a spirit stepped out of the shadows, blocking our path.

Deep claw marks covered the dead magician's face and neck, as if a wild animal had attacked him. Whole sections of flesh had been peeled from his broken body, but a tired velvet suit hid the worst of the damage.

The skin straining over the dybbuk's bones flashed through my mind—the way it looked like it didn't quite fit. My stomach convulsed.

Alara shook her head in disbelief.

"I tried to keep it safe," he said. "That was the only place I thought no one would find it. I never wanted it to get out." The spirit glanced at the cabinet that was burning up and vanishing without its magician. His arm shot out toward us. "May—"

I ripped the nail gun from my waistband and squeezed the trigger, sending a spray of cold-iron nails into his body. The magician exploded, sending tiny bits of purple velvet floating down over us.

23. MARKED

The black smoke rose from the building and sirens screamed in the distance as the van sped down the alley. Jared was stretched out on his back with his head in my lap. He rolled toward me, his arm falling around my waist. I brushed the hair away from his bruised face.

His eyelids fluttered.

He winced and pulled me closer, clutching the back of my shirt as his fingers trailed across my bare skin.

Jared blinked a few times before his blue eyes stared up at me, glassy and unfocused.

"Kennedy?" he mumbled, struggling to sit up. "What happened?"

Priest lifted one of the headphones away from his ear. "You got your butt kicked, that's what."

Lukas guided the van into a deserted gas station and climbed in the back with the rest of us. "You all right?" He held up three fingers. "How many do you see?"

"Nine." Jared swatted his hand away. "Now tell me what happened."

Alara started talking before anyone else had a chance. "Kennedy drew the Wall in the cabinet and bound the dybbuk inside."

"How did you know what it looked like?" Jared asked.

Alara answered for me. "She saw it in my journal."

"And you remembered it?"

Telling people for the first time was the worst part. My memory had always set me apart from other people, creating a boundary I couldn't cross. "I have eidetic memory—"

"It means photographic." Alara rushed on. "She can remember anything she sees and—"

"Not anything," I corrected. "Images and numbers mostly."

"Whatever." Alara waved off my denial. "You basically took out that thing alone. I singed it with a little holy water, but you did the rest."

I listened, barely registering the fact that Alara was talking about me. "She's exaggerating, but I did get these."

I opened my hand and revealed the green glass disks.

Alara smiled. "Like I said, I was just along for the ride."

It was strange to hear her bragging about me. Climbing in the well to help Priest had earned me a level of respect, but that was something anyone could've done. Drawing the Wall was different. It required skill and proved I finally had something to offer.

Priest reached for the disks and held them up to the light. "You found two?"

"It was dark and they looked exactly the same, so I grabbed them both."

"I'm not sure they'll do us much good," Lukas said. "The clue to finding the next piece is probably ash by now."

Priest closed his hand around the disks. "He's right. We found the other clues near the disks."

"Not all of them. The diagram of the Shift and the word *Lilburn* were in your journal, and parts of mine are encrypted. There has to be something—" Alara winced and pulled up her sleeve. "Oh my god."

Thin lines carved themselves into her skin, the same way Priest's mark had manifested after he destroyed Millicent's spirit. The impressions curved and one peaked into a triangle like the devil's tail from Andras' seal.

The fire Alara set must have burned through the cabinet and destroyed the dybbuk by now.

She reached in her pocket and rubbed her wrist with salt. Slowly, black lines filled the indentations. The guys pulled up their own sleeves, and Alara rubbed the crystals over their arms. The salt acted like the glass disks, illuminating a code invisible to the naked eye. The four of them positioned their wrists to form the seal, leaving only one small section missing.

I'm about to get my mark.

I hadn't realized how badly I wanted it—to be part of their secret world, and my mother's. To be one of them.

When did it change?

At Lilburn when Lukas saved my life, or in the well when Priest and I saved each other? When Alara trusted me to draw the Wall from memory? Or was it before that? When they lost almost everything they owned because of my mistake and still didn't turn their backs on me?

Maybe it was all of those moments layered between the White Stripes, a blue string, a voodoo medal, and the weight of Jared's eyes when he looked at me.

I inched my sleeve up slowly.

Will it hurt?

"Let's see it," Lukas said, the four of them still holding their arms together, waiting for the last Black Dove. I turned over my wrist so I could see the lines magically cutting themselves into my skin.

It was unmarked.

Confusion registered on their faces, mirroring my own.

"Wait," Priest said. "Alara's mark only showed up a second ago, and you shot the spirit on the way out. That had to be at least a few minutes after the fire destroyed the dybbuk. Give it some time."

Alara raised her eyes to meet mine. There was no way the fire could've burned through the box and destroyed the dybbuk before I shot the magician and we made it out of the building.

"I'm not one of you." I yanked my sleeve back down.

"What are you talking about?" Lukas sounded confused.

"Kennedy destroyed the vengeance spirit first." Alara's eyes dropped to the floor as though it was somehow her fault.

I wanted to disappear.

Instead, I threw open the door and ran.

The truth pounded me with every step. I wasn't destined to protect the world from a demon that murdered my mother, or the missing link the Legion needed to destroy him.

Halfway across the parking lot, a hand closed around my wrist. I spun around. Jared stared back at me, desperate and lost. "I didn't mean to grab you."

I wanted to tell him it was okay—that I needed someone to hold me until the pain melted away.

Someone who wouldn't let go.

I wasn't capable of saying the words, but Jared heard them anyway. He hooked a finger through my belt loop and tugged me closer. He kept his gaze locked on mine, and it felt like he could see the fears I was trying so hard to hide.

Can you see me?

Everything about his expression said yes. He closed the distance between us and wrapped his arms around me. I buried my face in his chest. Jared's hand slid under my hair, his thumb trailing along my neck.

I forgot how to breathe or think or do anything except hold on. "I'm not the one. I never was."

Jared's cheek brushed mine, as he whispered in my ear. "You're the only one."

A tear slid down my cheek. "You don't have to try to make me feel better."

"I want to."

"Why? I'm always screwing up and making things harder for you...." I bit my lip, wishing I hadn't said anything.

Jared pulled back so he could look at me, his hand still on my neck. "You think you make things harder for me?"

"I know I do."

"Only because I worry about you."

"You don't have to feel responsible for me," I said, my voice raw.

Jared ran his finger down my cheek, tracing the line where a tear had fallen. "That's not the reason."

I opened my hand and rested it against his chest without thinking. Jared's heart beat against my unmarked skin. "Half the time you won't even look at me."

His fingers slid down the back of my neck. "And the other half, I can't stop thinking about you."

I closed my hand, balling his shirt in my fist. "Jared—"

His face clouded over, and he stepped back. "I shouldn't have said anything. It was a mistake."

For a second, the words didn't register. Not when he just chased me and held me in his arms and said—

It was a mistake.

I was a mistake. That's what he meant.

This wasn't the first time I'd heard those words. Heat crawled up my neck where his hand had been a moment ago. I wanted to be anywhere but here—standing in front of the boy who didn't want me.

Jared reached for my arm, and I backed away, determined not to let him touch me again.

"Kennedy, you don't understand—"

I swallowed hard, struggling to find my voice. I didn't want him to know how much he'd hurt me. "There's nothing to understand."

I started to turn away.

Jared caught my hand again. "I didn't mean it the way it sounded. I know what I want." He bit his lip and stared at the gravel beneath our feet. "I just can't have it."

"Why not?"

Jared's blue eyes drifted back up to meet mine before he let my fingers slip out of his.

"I screw everything up, and the people close to me are the ones who get hurt." He shoved his hands in his pockets and nodded behind me. "Just ask Lukas."

I stood there paralyzed, as Lukas and Priest jogged toward us.

Lukas' smile faded, anger and jealousy warring in his eyes as he mentally calculated the distance between Jared and me. He had no way of knowing that we were miles apart in every way that mattered.

Priest didn't seem to notice. "We know you're one of us, Kennedy. I think we figured out why your mark didn't show up."

The mark.

Jared's rejection had temporarily distracted me from the fact that the universe had rejected me, too.

"We need to compare notes to be sure." Priest kept talking, but I was only half-listening. Jared wouldn't look at me, and Lukas wouldn't stop looking at his brother.

The words registered slowly. "Wait—you don't know how they work?"

Priest paced across the asphalt. "Our families didn't go into a lot of detail. It was sort of like 'destroy a vengeance spirit and you'll get your mark.'"

"That's pretty self-explanatory."

Lukas pushed his way past Jared. "There were lots of things they didn't tell us about, like the Shift, or the fact that one of the members of the Legion had dropped off the grid. This is probably another one of those things."

I thought about all the moments when the four of them seemed to be figuring things out as they went along. Their relatives probably never imagined they would all die on the same day, leaving the Legion in the hands of five teenagers who would have to ditch class to protect the world from a demon.

Lukas nudged my shoulder with his. "Come back and we'll explain why your mark didn't show up."

He sounded so sure.

But what if he was wrong?

Alara was sitting in the back of the van with the doors open, her journal resting in her lap. "Did you tell her?"

"Not yet." Priest hopped up next to her, buzzing with excitement. "So check it out. I got my mark after I destroyed Millicent's spirit in the well with the bolt I made, right?"

Lukas continued without missing a beat. "Mine showed up after I took out a Lady in White whose patterns I'd tracked for months."

Alara fidgeted with her eyebrow ring. "And my mark manifested because I used protective wards to take out the

211

dybbuk—holy water to drive it into the cabinet, and fire to destroy it."

"But I drew the Wall," I countered. "I helped."

"It doesn't matter," Priest said. "The fire's what actually destroyed it. Think about it. The bolt I made, the spirit Lukas tracked, Alara's wards..."

Jared's eyes lit up. "It makes sense."

"I'm glad it makes sense to someone," I mumbled.

"Weapons isn't your specialty," Priest continued. "The mark didn't show up because you shot the vengeance spirit with a gun."

"I don't understand."

He turned to Jared. "How'd you get yours?"

Jared closed his hand around the place where his mark lay dormant. "A cold-iron rod. I had the spirit in a headlock, and I drove the rod through his rib cage."

Alara rolled her eyes. "We wouldn't expect anything less."

I might still be one of them.

"But I don't have a specialty."

Alara raised her eyebrows. "You're kidding, right? You drew the Wall from memory."

My eidetic memory didn't seem like an impressive weapon in a battle against deadly spirits.

Priest shook his head. "More than that, the ability to draw symbols is directly related to invocation. Summoning and commanding angels and demons."

"I can definitely draw, but I can't summon anything—let alone an angel or a demon."

Priest looked right at me. "Then you're in luck because you don't have to invoke a vengeance spirit. You just have to kill one."

24. THE ONLY ONE

I stood outside the coffee shop and watched Lukas through the window as he paid the barista. After sleeping in the van all night, I would've killed to sink into one of the leather armchairs inside. But the shop was tiny, and even though we were fifty miles from Sunshine, the possibility of someone recognizing me was too high.

Standing out here was still better than being stuck in the van.

Priest and Jared had headed into town to pick up supplies as soon as they woke up, while Alara scoured the journals, searching for a clue that might lead to another piece of the Shift. She'd only lasted twenty minutes before she insisted on a caffeine run, and we jumped at the chance to see something other than the inside of the van.

Lukas came back out with a cardboard drink carrier and handed me a steaming cup. "This one's yours."

"Thanks." I took a sip. "You put cinnamon in it."

He shrugged. "I remembered you like it."

Of course he did.

Lukas walked down the street and I fell in step next to him. "Is everything okay?"

He gave me a weak smile. "You mean besides almost getting killed and setting a store on fire?"

"It feels like you're mad at me."

Lukas took his coin out of his pocket and rolled it over his fingers a few times before he answered. "I'm not mad. Just disappointed. I didn't think Jared would have a chance with you. You're not like the girls who usually fall for him."

My stomach lurched.

How many girls was he talking about?

Heat spread through my cheeks. I sped up, hoping Lukas wouldn't notice me blushing.

"Kennedy!" Lukas yanked my arm so hard that it felt like my shoulder was coming out of the socket.

A car horn blared and tires skidded.

Lukas hauled me back onto the sidewalk, and I fell against his chest, and he folded his arms around me. For a second, I was too scared to move. He stepped back and held me at arm's length. "Are you okay?"

I nodded, watching as the coffee seeped out of the cups and into the street.

Lukas shook his head. "I'm a jerk. I shouldn't have said anything."

"You're not the jerk."

He pushed the hair away from my face. "I just don't want to see you get hurt."

I couldn't look at him. "Don't worry. I won't."

His silver coin was lying on the sidewalk. I bent down to pick it up, studying it for the first time.

"It belonged to my dad. It was the one thing he gave to me instead of Jared."

In the center of the coin, a dove perched on a limb with five branches. A phrase was stamped around the circumference of the coin, in a language I couldn't place.

"It's Italian. It says, 'May the black dove always carry you.'"

I turned the coin over so I could see the other side.

It was exactly the same.

⊣ • ⊢

After a second coffee run, we finally made it back to the van. Jared was sitting on the hood sorting through a bag from the sporting goods store with Priest.

"You guys were gone a long time." Jared tried to hide the edge in his voice. "I thought someone recognized you again."

I walked past him. "We were talking."

"Well, we've been waiting." He made an attempt to

216

sound casual, but failed miserably. "Alara found something and she wants to show all of us at the same time."

Alara was sitting on the grass with the journals spread out around her.

"So what have you got?" Priest asked.

"Take a look." She opened Jared's journal to a page covered in rows of letters with blank spaces between them.

Jared sighed. "That's been there forever. It's an old encryption technique. You leave out every other letter in each word. But it's not easy to crack because the words aren't separated, so the pattern's hard to figure out. Lukas already tried."

"What if we don't need to identify the pattern?" The hint of a smile played on Alara's lips.

Priest leaned over the page. "There's no other way to decipher it."

"Remember when you said that each shade of glass could be used to reveal a different layer of the infrared spectrum?" Alara uncurled her fingers. The two green disks from the magic shop rested in her palm. "I tried it with some random pages in our journals."

She ran one of the disks over the code in Lukas' journal. The missing letters appeared as if they had been written in invisible ink. The letters were still strung together without any breaks, but they were all there. Alara held up the disk and tossed the fake into the grass. "Turns out, this one's the real thing."

Lukas' jaw dropped. "Get me some paper."

Alara dictated the letters while Lukas transcribed them. Within minutes, the page was covered and his pen still hadn't stopped moving.

"What does it say?" Priest leaned over Lukas' shoulder, the Beastie Boys' "No Sleep Till Brooklyn" blasting from his headphones. He nodded in time with the beat as Lukas slashed lines between the letters to separate the words.

When he finished, Lukas turned the journal around. "Take a look."

derek / lockhart
the piece is hidden where most will
never dare to look / in the hands of its
guardian who most will never pass / but
if you are reading this the task remains
the same / remember the lessons from
others who have tried to steal from the
dead / no one will ever get it out of
hearts of mercy / may the black dove
always carry you

Alara added a few more packets of sugar to her coffee. "That's encouraging."

"Ever heard of Hearts of Mercy?" Priest asked.

Lukas took out his cell and started typing. "It has to be a place."

Alara picked at her silver nail polish. "You sure about that?"

"All the other clues referred to places," he said. "I've already got some hits."

I wasn't listening anymore. I couldn't stop thinking about the part of the message none of them were talking about.

Remember the lessons from others who have tried to steal from the dead. No one will ever get it out of Hearts of Mercy.

⊰ • ⊱

"The family of five was discovered late last night after a neighbor reported gunshots." The newscaster's voice crackled over the van's radio. "This is the third multiple homicide in western Montgomery County in the last two weeks. In an official statement this morning, Police Chief Montano stated that this level of violence is unprecedented. Frightened citizens are looking for answers."

It was the second report chronicling an incident of violent crime in less than an hour.

Lukas turned off the radio. "Either we're getting closer to the Marrow, or a crapload of criminals all decided to move to the same area."

Jared guided the van along the narrow back roads that twisted through the woods. "I just hope you're right about where we're going."

"The children's home is the only Hearts of Mercy

within two hundred miles," Lukas said. "And judging from what happened in that place, the disk will be there."

Priest dumped out the bag from the sporting goods store, and a pile of guns clattered onto the floor. "Don't worry. I've got us covered."

"Someone sold you those?" I asked. Priest didn't look old enough to buy a lottery ticket.

"Paintball guns." He held up a black military-style model. "Close range with a laser sight." Priest opened a package of gray plastic balls. "I'm going to fill the cases with holy water and agrimony instead of paint."

Alara examined one of the cases. "Not unless you grabbed a jar of agrimony from the warehouse."

"Is there anything else we can use?"

She picked up a silver double-barreled pistol that matched her nail polish. "Rock salt and cloves should do the trick. They both repel spirits."

Priest leaned over the front seat. "Can you find a market and a hardware store? I still need a caulking gun, fireplace lighters, and hair spray. You know, the basics."

"Planning a little home improvement?" Alara teased.

Priest started sketching a weapon design on a sheet of paper. "Something like that."

⊣ • ⊢

Priest tossed the tenth silver can into the shopping cart. We were in the grocery store picking up the supplies he needed for whatever he was making, a detail he refused to share.

"What exactly are you going to do with all that hair spray?" I kept my voice down, careful to hide my face under the folds of Priest's gigantic hoodie.

"Inventors never reveal their secrets." He crossed another item off the list written on his hand.

"I thought that was magicians."

He grabbed a few rolls of duct tape, the staple of his arsenal. "Same rule applies."

"Should we get extra cloves?"

Alara had already purchased a basketful and retreated to the van with Lukas to fill the paintball cases, and Jared was at the hardware store looking for a caulking gun that met Priest's specifications. We were in charge of everything else on the list.

Priest shrugged. "Might as well."

I pushed the cart as he tossed a few fireplace starters inside. "You said you grew up in Northern California, right?"

"Yeah. Near Berkeley."

"With your parents?" After Alara's story, I hoped grandparents hijacking their grandchildren for training wasn't the norm.

Priest ticked the items off on his fingers, mentally totaling our purchases. "My parents died in a car accident when I was three. My granddad raised me."

"I'm sorry."

"I don't really remember my mom and dad, but he talked about them all the time."

We walked down the cereal aisle, and Priest grabbed a box of Lucky Charms. "Don't tell Alara. These aren't on the approved shopping list."

I stared at the red box, remembering the first time my mom pulled one just like it out of a grocery bag in our kitchen.

We sat cross-legged on the living room floor as she dumped the cereal into a giant glass bowl. Then she handed me a smaller bowl. "We're going to pick all the colored marshmallows out of the cereal and put them in your bowl, okay?"

"Then what?"

She laughed and popped one of the marshmallows in my mouth. "We eat them."

"Kennedy?" Priest stared back at me. He was halfway up the aisle and I was standing in exactly the same spot.

"Sorry. What else do we need?"

He checked his hand again. "Glass cleaner, a novena candle, matches, and shortening."

"Shortening?"

"It's basically grease. Cheap WD-40."

I made a mental note never to eat anything with shortening in it again.

I wondered what he could possibly make with this junk. "I can't believe your grandfather taught you how to do all this."

"He taught me everything." Priest opened the Lucky Charms and picked out a few marshmallows. He offered me the box, but I only shook my head. "I was home-schooled. Half the day was the state curriculum on steroids, and the other half was mechanical engineering, physics, and basic Legion stuff."

Priest didn't seem like the handful of homeschooled kids I knew back home, who were still catching up on TV shows from the last two decades. At my high school, he would've been in all the advanced placement classes, but instead of hanging out with the valedictorian hopefuls, he probably would've opted for the skaters. It wasn't hard to picture him in the hall wearing his headphones and dee-jaying parties on the weekends.

"So you always knew you'd be in the Legion?"

"Yeah. I was an only child, and my cousins are all pretty stupid. My granddad wouldn't let them change the batteries in a remote." He shook the box, searching for more charms.

"I wish I had grown up knowing the truth about my part in all this. If there's really anything to know."

Priest stopped walking. "The truth is relative. Maybe your mom was going to tell you, but she died before she had the chance."

I wanted to believe that so badly.

He popped another handful of charms in his mouth and smiled. "So Jared, huh?"

"What?" I tried to sound shocked.

Priest shrugged. "If you don't wanna talk about it, I get it."

"There's nothing to talk about. Trust me."

"Nobody else knows if that's what you're worried about. I'm a lot more perceptive than the rest of them, a result of my superior education and high IQ," he said sarcastically.

I didn't know how to explain my feelings for Jared, or if I should try.

"Jared doesn't care about me." I emptied the contents of the cart onto a conveyor belt.

Priest tilted his head. "You sure about that?"

I was afraid to consider the alternative. "I can't afford to take any more chances. I'm trying to hold it together."

Priest gave me a knowing look. "Maybe you're not the only one."

25. HEARTS OF MERCY

A layer of black dust coated the windows that weren't shattered. An oxidized plaque on the stone building confirmed we were in the right place: HEARTS OF MERCY HOME FOR CHILDREN.

Behind the iron gates, the yard was a tangle of weeds and rat-infested ivy that snaked up the sides of the chipped stone.

This place looked more like a prison than an orphanage, from the rusted playground merry-go-round to the rotted weeping willow split down the center.

Something lay in the dirt—a book, bound in faded cloth. I picked it up and brushed off the cover.

The Secret Garden.

My chest tightened and the book slipped from my

hand, loose pages fluttering to the ground. My dad read me the story when I was too young to understand most of it, but I remembered the title, and I'd still never read it.

"Kennedy?" Lukas looked worried. "What's wrong?"

My eyes rested on the book for a second before I walked away. "Nothing."

Jared passed out the gear. "We've gotta be careful inside. Lots of kids died here, and some of their spirits are probably still hanging around."

A single palm print was branded in the center of one of the windowpanes.

"How did they die?" I asked.

Lukas slung a paintball gun over his shoulder. "The articles said it was an outbreak of meningitis."

Jared tossed us each a two-way radio and a pack of batteries. More supplies from the sporting goods store. "Priest rigged them with splitters so we can stay in touch. If we can keep the batteries charged."

I shoved the extra batteries in the pocket of my cargo pants. "Why wouldn't they stay charged?"

Priest unscrewed the back of his EMF detector and swapped out the double As. "Spirits absorb the energy from things around them, including batteries. If this place has more than a couple inside, we'll burn through these fast."

"Lukas, take Priest and Alara and check out the attic and the second floor." Jared loaded the black paintball gun. "Kennedy and I will take the first floor and the basement. We call in every twenty minutes. If the radios die, we meet by the front door after a half hour."

Everyone collected their gear except Lukas. "Why is she going with you?"

Jared didn't take the bait. "What difference does it make?"

"If it doesn't matter, then she can come with us."

"Because you did such a great job of looking out for her last time?" Jared turned his back on Lukas and waved me over. "Let's go."

Lukas flinched. "I guess nothing could happen to her with you around? Because you never screw up."

Jared froze and the color drained from his face. Lukas was referring to something specific.

I stepped in front of Jared, unwilling to be a pawn in their game. "Don't talk about me like I'm not here. I'm a big girl. What happened wasn't Lukas' fault."

Jared stalked toward the orphanage's cracked concrete steps.

"Come on. Let's go," Lukas said.

I waited until Jared was out of earshot. "I'm going with Jared this time. He can't go in there when he's angry, or he'll be distracted. That's dangerous."

Lukas' face fell, but he forced a smile anyway and tucked a stray strand of hair behind my ear. "Be careful."

"I will."

Jared waited at the front door with Priest and Alara. The rotted wood didn't offer much resistance, and he forced it open easily.

"Catch you later," Priest called as he climbed the staircase with Lukas and Alara.

The first floor was dark, with patches of light slipping through the scum-covered windows. A moth-eaten yellow sofa surrounded by empty beer cans and cigarette butts was all that was left of the living room. A rat scurried across the floor and I jumped, bumping into Jared.

"Sorry," I mumbled.

He switched on a flashlight, and I followed him to the kitchen.

A small window over the stained white sink was coated in a decade's worth of grease and provided the only natural light. Linoleum squares peeled up from the floor like the curling edges of burnt paper. The pattern of decay led to the pantry door. It was slightly ajar, ruined and warped like everything else in this place. I nudged it with my boot.

The door creaked open.

I froze. "Jared—"

A little girl sat on the floor in a filthy brown nightgown, hugging her knees to her chest. Huge, tormented brown eyes stared past me as if I wasn't there. She rocked herself gently, her frail body lost in the folds of fabric. Unlike the full body apparitions I'd encountered, she was hazy and faded.

I backed up slowly.

The child didn't look away from a spot somewhere beyond me.

Jared caught my elbow. "She's a residual spirit, energy left behind after the person moves on. She can't hurt you."

"I think I'll keep my distance anyway."

Even if we didn't find a single vengeance spirit within these walls, this place was filled with ghosts—remnants of the terrible things that must've happened here. Things I could see as clearly as the broken windows outside.

Jared opened the next pantry door and I tensed, expecting to see the face of another lost child. This one was stacked floor to ceiling with vacuum-sealed pallets. Jared bent down and wiped the dust off the thick plastic. I read the labels underneath and gagged.

Dog food—cans and cans of it—towering to the ceiling. Enough to feed fifty dogs.

Or fifty children.

Jared kicked the stack. "My dad used to say the evil we enact on each other is worse than anything spirits and demons can do to us." He picked up a dented can of dog food and chucked it against the wall, brown slop splattering across the wallpaper. "I never believed him until now."

Static crackled over Jared's radio. "It's Priest. You guys okay?"

"We're good," he said. "Find anything up there?"

"Not yet. Check with you in twenty."

Jared shoved the radio in his back pocket. "Let's see if there's anything in the basement."

I couldn't get out of the kitchen fast enough. The residue of despair clung to my skin like the filth coating the windows. We needed to find the next piece of the Shift and get out of this house.

The basement door was tucked under the staircase, secured by two heavy dead bolts at the top, far above the reach of a child.

I couldn't imagine the terror of being locked in a basement. My pulse raced as Jared unlocked the door. The splintered wooden stairs disappeared into a sea of black.

He used his flashlight to navigate the cracks in the steps. "Stay close."

"Not a problem." I had no intention of getting lost down there.

At the base of the staircase, it was impossible to see more than a few feet. I grabbed Jared's hand without thinking, terrified we might get separated.

A corridor stretched beyond us, but it looked more like a tunnel. "I think it leads to another room."

Jared shined the light along the walls, and I shuddered. Drawings covered the lower sections—childish depictions of rectangular houses with triangle roofs, and stick-figure families that morphed into more sinister images. Children crying as monsters towered over them, with gnashing teeth and razor-sharp claws.

When the corridor opened up into an enormous room, the temperature dropped, and cold air crawled over my skin. I squeezed Jared's hand tighter, my pride back at the top of the stairs along with my courage.

A bare bulb flickered at the opposite end of the room, revealing the truth about this place in weak bursts. They stood in two rows at the ends of the aluminum beds that were outfitted with thin mattresses and frayed canvas straps:

Children. At least twenty of them.

Ranging from four or five years old to nine or ten, they were all sickly and gaunt, in matching pairs of stained long underwear. With their hair buzzed to less than an inch, it was hard to distinguish the boys from the girls. Their eyes reflected the light when it hit them, as though they were still among the living.

But something was wrong with their faces.

The muscles were frozen, contorted in unnatural expressions and exaggerated smiles. Only their eyes moved, conveying the emotions their faces couldn't.

"Turn around slowly." Jared kept his voice low. "We're going back the way we came."

"No, we aren't."

I glanced at two children standing behind me. They watched us curiously, their faces as mangled as the others'. They held hands, the taller one clutching the younger child's protectively. Steel gray eyes and innocent blue ones gazed back at us.

Jared pulled me closer.

The taller child lifted a thin arm. A plastic IV port was taped inside the crook of his bony elbow. He pointed at the other end of the room, where the remaining children were lined up.

"What do they want?"

Jared pulled my hand behind his back and drew me closer. "Something happened here. I think they need us to bear witness so they can rest."

The child was still pointing.

"Should we do what he wants?"

"Spirits of children are unpredictable, but I don't think we have a choice. There are too many of them. If they get agitated…"

I nodded. "Let's go."

Turning my back on those children-that-weren't-children was terrifying. I kept thinking about the girl in the yellow dress at Lilburn, who had looked so innocent right before she tried to kill us.

We walked closer as the flickering bulb bathed the room in pale light. An IV pole was positioned at the head of each dented bed frame, the canvas straps pulled tight across the stripped mattresses, as if they were still restraining bodies beneath them.

Yellowed newspaper clippings were taped to the walls. I scanned the chilling headlines: *Seven Children Die in West Virginia Group Home, Siblings Acquitted for Poi-*

soning Their Parents After Years of Abuse, Nurse in Har-
ken Fired for Administering Lethal Dose of Medication.

I couldn't stand to read any more.

I looked back at the rows of hopeful eyes. Without a word, each child extended an arm. A piece of tape secured an IV port inside every elbow. One of the frailer children handed me an amber bottle with block lettering typed on the yellow label: STRYCHNINE.

Jared rubbed his free hand over his face. "Strychnine causes muscular damage—" As he spoke the words, their eyes widened. "They were poisoned."

Bile rose in the back of my throat. "And those people got away with it."

"No," Jared said, his eyes full of anger. "My dad used to say the evidence of evil can be hidden, but it always leaves a stain. We'll tell someone what happened here."

The older child behind me walked toward the other children, beckoning us to follow.

We reached the last bed.

The wall behind it was cracked, like someone had tried to break through. A hole about the size of a small doorway revealed the wooden framework within the wall, and the brick behind it. Whoever started the hole had never finished it.

I heard a sound. It started out faint and intensified. "Is that—?"

"Scratching."

It was coming from inside the wall.

The kids around us scattered, cowering behind the aluminum frames of their beds. A figure emerged from the hole.

A boy.

He was older than the rest of the children—maybe thirteen or fourteen. It was hard to tell, but he was much taller than the others, with sharper features and vacant eyes. A sledgehammer rested against his shoulder.

He stepped closer, his clothes coated with dust and debris from the crumbling bits of concrete. "I tried to find a way out, I swear. But the brick was too thick." The boy's voice wavered, a crazed look in his bloodshot eyes. "Now I'm the only one left."

Did he think he was still alive?

"Father will be angry if he finds out you were down here. He'll punish me." The spirit paced back and forth in front of us, muttering to himself.

"He's gone," Jared said. "You don't have to worry about him anymore."

The spirit's eyes narrowed. "Strangers lie. If I watch over what's his, he'll come back for me. He promised."

The boy had to be referring to the other children. Was he responsible for keeping them down here until his deranged father killed them?

Jared raised the semiautomatic paintball gun, shoving

me behind him. The spirit vanished as the paintball cases exploded against the wall, brown holy water running down it in streaks.

An arm swung around my neck from behind. The point of something thin and sharp pressed against the skin below my ear.

A needle.

Every breath brought the point closer, and I imagined it puncturing my skin and filling my body with the poison that probably killed every child in this room.

Jared tossed the gun. It spun over the footprints on the concrete floor. "Don't hurt her. I'll do whatever you want."

The spirit's hand moved as he spoke and the needle threatened to puncture my skin. "I have to protect it. Then I'll be free."

"I can get you out of here," Jared pleaded.

"It's too late for that," the boy whispered in my ear, the warmth of breath absent. He pushed me forward without compromising his grip. "Move."

Jared backed up slowly without taking his eyes off me.

The spirit tightened his arm around my neck and nodded from Jared to the crumbling hole in the wall. "Get inside."

Jared stepped into the hole without hesitating, a doorway leading nowhere. I waited, praying I wouldn't feel the prick of the needle on my skin.

A second passed, then another.

One hard shove and I stumbled into the crude opening. Jared pulled me toward him. We were trapped in a cage of wooden framework no bigger than a phone booth, with nothing but solid brick behind it.

Jared locked his arms around my waist. "You're okay."

I looked up at him in time to see his expression change from relief to terror. He spun me around so that my back was against the brick wall. Now I was facing the hole. Jared's body wedged between the vicious spirit and me.

"What are you—" I gasped as a board smacked against the opening, and nails pounded into the wood. "He's closing the hole."

My throat closed along with it. The darkness, the memory, the terror closed in on me. Dizziness tugged at my equilibrium.

Another board hit the wall.

"No!" I threw my hands against it, pushing with all my strength. The wood vibrated each time the hammer hit a nail. Jared turned around so we were both facing the slices of the room that were still visible.

I couldn't see the spirits of the other children anymore, only glimpses of the bare bulb and the head of the hammer.

Jared pounded his fists on the slats of wood, but they didn't give. "The nails shouldn't be this strong."

The sledgehammer hit another nail.

236

The sound reminded me of the bolts hitting the floor of the warehouse when they had unscrewed themselves from the window. It had been impossible for Lukas and Jared to hold them in place.

Was the boy's spirit strengthening these nails the same way?

Another board slapped against the opening, eclipsing the last sliver of light. The hammer hit the wood over and over. I counted every nail.

Twenty-seven.

That was the count when the last one plunged into the wood, trapping us inside.

26. WITHIN THE WALLS

*H*e *shut us in. He shut us in. He shut us in.*
I heard myself screaming, but the only words I could make out were the ones in my head.

I was back inside my mother's closet again, helpless and terrified—the memories battering me one after another. Darkness pressing in from all sides, heavy and suffocating. My ragged breathing. The smell of mothballs and cedar. Smooth wood under my hands as I ran them over the walls.

Now I was trapped again.

I clawed at the wood, splinters digging underneath my fingernails and shredding my skin. Ignoring the pain, I pounded and prayed for one of the boards to break. Though I could barely see him, I felt Jared's hands scratching and banging alongside mine.

"How are we going to get out?" My voice echoed back at me.

"The nails are too strong. He must be holding them in place."

Jared stopped fighting and turned to face me. He wrapped his arms around my neck and pulled me against him. "It's gonna be okay." He tried to sound convincing, but our bodies were too close to lie. His heart was pounding even harder than mine.

My head rested against Jared's chest, and I listened to the sound of his breathing. It was too fast, like his heartbeat.

He leaned down, his mouth on my ear. "I'm not gonna let anything happen to you. I'll get us out of this. I promise."

I took a deep breath, my face still buried in his shirt. "Don't make promises you can't keep."

He took my face in his hands and raised my chin with his thumb. "I want you to know I'd never do that."

I nodded, too frightened to know anything.

"Give me your radio," he said. "I dropped mine fighting with the dead kid."

I dug it out of my pocket and slid it between us. Jared rested his arms around my neck, toying with the dials. He pressed the button over and over, repeating the same thing. "Lukas? Priest? Alara? Anyone there?"

"We're inside a wall. You won't get any reception." I squeezed my eyes shut, trying not to cry.

"It doesn't matter. When we don't show up, they'll look for us."

I shook my head and tears spilled down my cheeks. "I don't want them to."

"Why not?"

If they came down here, they might get hurt. There were so many spirits and no way to predict what could happen if those traumatized children felt threatened. The boy with the sledgehammer had probably been as docile as the rest of them once.

I pressed my face against Jared's chest and tried to catch my breath.

"Kennedy, are you crying?" He pulled back, trying to look at me even though there was no way he could see me in the dark.

"No."

He pulled me tighter, resting his chin on the top of my head. "I'm so sorry. I should've let you go with Lukas."

"There's no way you could have known."

Jared took a shuddering breath. "He's the better half. I'm the screwup. No matter what I do."

I laid my palms against his chest. "You protect everyone."

His breath caught and the person who seemed so unbreakable finally broke.

"Is that what you think? If you knew the truth, you'd

never say that. I screwed up. Worse than this." His chest heaved. "Worse than anything."

I reached up and touched his damp cheeks. "It can't be that bad—"

Jared caught my wrists in his hands and held them tight. "It is that bad. *I'm* that bad. If you knew what I did, you wouldn't want to touch me or be anywhere near me."

He was coming apart, the way I had so many times. "That's not true. Whatever it is—"

Jared exploded. "I killed our parents—yours, mine, all of them. It's my fault they're dead. Do you want to be close to me now?"

I heard the words, but they didn't make sense. "What are you talking about? You didn't even know my mom."

"No. But I wanted to." Jared pressed his face into my hands, still holding my wrists. "I wanted to find all the members of the Legion. I thought they'd be stronger together, like the journals say. I didn't believe my dad when he told me Andras was always hunting them—that it was too risky. So I started researching on my own, piecing together information from conversations I overheard between my dad and my uncle with things my father had told me. If I didn't have two family members in the Legion, I probably never would've figured it out. But I found them all. Even your mom, the one nobody else could find."

"How?"

"My uncle was looking for the member who dropped

241

off the grid. One day, I heard him tell my dad that he'd figured out she was a woman, living in the DC area with her daughter. I went through his desk and found her name—and yours."

"What are you saying?" My voice sounded distant and muffled, like it belonged to someone else and I was eavesdropping on the conversation.

Jared's tears ran down my hands. "I made a list of all the names. I was gonna show it to my dad. The next day, he was dead. They were all dead. And suddenly we were the Legion."

It's his fault my mom is dead.

I knew it was true, but I couldn't hate him.

Jared's father hid something from him, and he went looking for answers. How many times had I searched for the note my father wrote, the one I saw perfectly every time I closed my eyes? My mother had never let me see it again after the day he left, and it had only made me search harder.

I would have looked for them, too.

My body shook as I cried. This time I couldn't pretend, and I couldn't stop. Jared let go of my wrists, trying to create space between us, but it was impossible.

There was no space between us—inside or outside these walls.

"I know you'll never be able to forgive me. My own brother hates me," he said.

It all made sense. The tension between them—the

unspoken anger simmering below the surface—it was about so much more than their father choosing Jared to take his place in the Legion...or me.

"I'm sorry. I wish I could take it back," Jared whispered, his voice hoarse. "All I want to do is be near you, and I don't deserve to be."

"What?"

"I'm sorry—"

I shook my head. "No. The other thing."

Jared stilled and put his hands flat against the boards behind me, with my face between them. I couldn't see him in the darkness, but I could feel him watching me cry.

Seeing me—the person I tried so hard to hide from the world and replace with someone better.

"All I want to do is be near you." He spoke the words slowly, his face so close I could feel his breath on my skin and smell the salt on his. "Kennedy, what do you want?"

The question lingered between us, tearing me apart. But I couldn't make myself say the words, no matter how many times I repeated them in my head. "It doesn't make a difference."

"It makes a difference to me." His voice was raw and deep.

"I want to matter. I want to be the kind of girl someone can't just walk away from and forget."

He ran his thumb down the center of my bottom lip. "No one could ever forget you."

Someone did.

Something inside me gave way, and I started sobbing.

Jared took my face in his hands and his lips brushed mine. It wasn't a kiss. It was a breath. A heartbeat.

"You see what I want you to see. It has nothing to do with who I really am," I said, our lips barely separated.

"Then let me see the rest," he whispered.

I shook my head, choking on my tears. "I can't."

He pressed his forehead against mine. "Why not?"

"Because I'm afraid I won't be able to go back to the person I was when you walk away." I said it before I could stop myself, before I calculated all the ways those words could hurt me.

His hands slid behind my neck, tangling in my hair. "I won't walk away."

"Everyone does, eventually."

He gathered me up in his arms and held me tighter than anyone ever had. Tight enough to make me forget about where we were, or how much I wanted to be someone else. In this moment, I wanted to be me. The girl Jared was holding.

I wanted right now.

"I don't know how anyone could walk away from you," he murmured. "How anyone could stand to hurt you."

Easily.

"I want…" He hesitated. "Can I kiss you?"

I pushed up onto my toes and pressed my mouth

244

against his, opening into him. He pulled me closer. His body melted against mine, and my breath hitched as Jared's finger trailed down my throat. I tugged on his bottom lip and he kissed me harder, like it didn't matter if we ever got out of here.

I leaned into him, my hands crushed between his back and the boards.

"Kennedy." His voice was ragged, his fingers slipping under the bottom of my shirt. I felt his chest rising and falling, the pressure of all the things we couldn't say in every kiss.

27. UNEARTHED

Something vibrated on the other side of the wall. Was the spirit nailing in another board?

It intensified, and a piece of wood started to give. I pulled back as the board behind Jared's shoulders came loose, and light flooded through the crack.

"You guys okay?" Priest's voice pierced the haze and I turned toward it, blinking hard against the light.

Jared stared back at me, his face streaked with the blood from my hands.

Lukas stood on the other side holding the dislodged board. His eyes dropped to Jared's hands still resting on my hips, and his expression darkened.

Jared stepped back awkwardly. "We're good. Just get her out."

Lukas and Priest tore the boards away one at a time until the opening was big enough to climb through.

I stepped out and Alara threw her arms around me. I winced and she drew back. "Oh my god, Kennedy. Look at your hands."

I didn't want to see them. I wanted to remember them touching Jared's face and wiping his tears, instead of clawing at the boards.

"How did you find us?"

Broken glow sticks bathed the room in green light. Alara pointed at the rows of beds. The spirits of the children gathered in the aisle, except for the one that trapped us inside the wall. He was conspicuously missing, his sledgehammer lying at the foot of one of the beds.

"They showed us where you were," she said.

I stared out into the sea of expectant faces. "Thank you."

Would they be able to move on now? I hated the thought of them being trapped in this slaughterhouse.

"What happened to the other one?" I asked.

Priest held up the nail gun loaded with the cold-iron nails. "I took him out."

Jared leaned against the wall, his head down. "Did you find the disk?"

"There was nothing up there except rats and empty beer bottles," Alara answered.

"We can't leave until we find it." Jared's eyes drifted to the hole. "Not after that."

Jared rubbed his hand over his face. Now that I knew the truth about the secret Jared was carrying, I could see the guilt in his every movement.

Priest paced the room. "If you were going to hide something in this house, where would you put it?"

"Down here," I answered automatically. "Not many people would hang around long enough to find it."

Priest looked at the spirits. "Think they'll mind if we try?"

⊰ • ⊱

Sifting through the evidence of a mass-murder scene was harder than I expected, especially when the victims were scampering around us. I lifted the thin mattresses easily, working the right side of the room while Alara worked the left. Jared and Lukas checked the walls for cracks and hidden spaces while two of the taller children trailed behind them.

Priest sat on the floor with a handheld transistor radio. A group of spirits gathered around him.

"In the mood for some music?" I asked.

"Just the opposite." He turned the dial until a steady stream of static crackled through the air, then he cranked the volume all the way up.

"What are you doing?"

He smiled and pulled a calculator out of his jeans. "Watch and learn."

"You really do carry that thing around all the time."

"Standard operating genius procedure." Priest turned on the calculator and held it against the radio until it emitted a loud tone. "You can use calculators to make all sorts of stuff. Can you see if there's any tape around?"

A tray next to one of the beds held a dirty roll of medical tape—the same kind securing the IV ports onto the spirits' arms. I tossed it to Priest, eager to have it out of my hands. "Will this work?"

"Yep."

Lukas came over to take a look. "What are you making?"

Priest held up the contraption. "Behold, all of you scientifically challenged." He took a few nails out of his pocket and held them next to the calculator. The radio emitted another low tone. "What we have here is a metal detector."

"You're kidding, right?" Lukas asked.

"Did you miss my little demonstration?" Priest stood up. The spirits scattered, watching from a safe distance.

He walked back to the mouth of the corridor and reentered the room, sweeping it slowly. Each time he passed a metal tray or an IV pole, the radio emitted the same sound. Like most of Priest's inventions, the construction reminded me of a futuristic science-fair project. But it was completely functional, and the spirits were mesmerized. Every few minutes, the station changed suddenly.

Alara's eyes widened. "They're channeling the electrical energy."

"Come on, kids. I'm working here." Priest swept the metal detector around the last bed. When it didn't pick up anything new, he glanced at the hole. "Should we check in there?"

I shuddered at the thought as the device transmitted another tone.

The sledgehammer rested at the end of the bed next to Priest.

"So much for science." He lifted it by the handle and smacked the head of the hammer against his hand. "I wonder if I could replace this with cold iron? It's already loose."

"Probably from being used to seal us up in a wall," I said sarcastically. I didn't want that thing to become a modified weapon in our arsenal.

Priest twisted the head and it hit the ground, cracking the concrete floor.

"It's a sign." Alara picked it up and walked toward the hole, ready to toss it inside. But she stopped short. "Priest?"

He took the hunk of metal from her and examined the circular groove where it connected to the handle. A large plate lay behind it with a channel cut through the center. Priest used his screwdriver to remove the plate, exposing a circular chamber. A disk's silver edge rested against the lip, completely protected.

He flipped over the head of the hammer, and the circle of yellow glass dropped into his hand.

Alara gasped. "How did someone get it in there without that vengeance spirit going crazy?"

"Maybe they gave him something he wanted."

Jared picked up the handle off the floor. Numbers were scratched into the wood. "What do you think they mean? It looks like math homework."

39.9159082-80.7420296

Lukas jerked the handle out of his brother's hand, studying the numbers. "They're coordinates."

"You think they lead to the last piece of the Shift?" Alara asked.

Lukas tightened his hand around the splintered wood. "Yeah. And if we find it, we can destroy Andras."

"Let's get out of here." Priest handed the metal detector to one of the spirits. The child grabbed it and scampered away.

We walked back down the aisle between the beds. The children were already playing with the metal detector, possibly the only toy some of them had ever seen. We moved past the nightmarish drawings and up the cracked stairs. I thought about all the innocent people the Legion must have saved over the years, and I couldn't help but wonder...

Who saved the innocent souls?

28. FLORIDA WATER

I waited on the front steps, hoping to avoid the awkwardness of being alone with Lukas and Jared. Priest and Alara had disappeared the moment we left the basement. Priest was determined to figure out where the coordinates on the handle led, and Alara had mumbled something about tying up loose ends.

I stared at my hands, splinters and dirt embedded under my nails instead of black charcoal. Artists protected their hands. What did that say about me? How much would I have to give up for the Legion?

The muffled sound of voices rose inside the house. Without any vengeance spirits to fight, Lukas and Jared were left with each other. A door slammed and snippets of their conversation drifted outside.

"We both know you don't care about her," Lukas shouted. "She's just something else for you to take—"

A knot formed in the pit of my stomach. Lukas meant something to me, even if I couldn't define exactly what it was. I didn't want to hurt him.

"Luke, I didn't mean for this to happen—"

"Like you didn't mean to kill Dad?" The words echoed through the house, layered with pain and anger.

"You know that was an accident," Jared said quietly.

"Everything's an accident with you because you never think about anyone but yourself." I leaned against the door debating whether or not to open it. "Is Kennedy going to be your next victim?"

"Hey, are you going back in?" Alara climbed the stairs behind me, a canvas knapsack slung over her shoulder.

"Wait—"

She opened the door before I could stop her, catching Lukas and Jared off guard. They both turned and looked past Alara to where I stood. I dropped my eyes, hoping they wouldn't realize how much I'd heard.

Alara broke the silence. "Am I interrupting something that looks like it needs interrupting?"

Jared slouched against the wall, his eyes glued to the floor.

Lukas noticed Alara's knapsack. "What are you doing?"

She strode past them. "My grandmother would never

254

leave the spirits of those children in this awful place. I have to try to release them so they can move on."

"Can you do that?" I followed her tentatively.

"I'm not sure. I've only seen my grandmother do it, and I don't have the traditional supplies. But I think I can make some substitutions."

"Why didn't the spirits disappear like the little boy in the well?" I asked. He had seemed at peace.

"Sometimes they don't know how to move on. They're lost and need help finding their way."

Lukas frowned. "And you're going to be their guide?"

"More like their travel agent." Alara pulled four packages of Red Cap tobacco out of her bag. "If you guys want to help, I'm going to need a bucket."

The spirits crowded around Alara as she emptied one of the tobacco packets into a bucket of water and stirred it with her hand. "We have to make a floor wash and cleanse the room of negative energy or the loas won't come."

"The what?"

"The loas are intermediaries in the spirit world. Some of them guide lost souls to the other side," she explained, her arms soaked to the elbows. "But they won't show up unless we scrub this room down."

Jared studied the brown water. "And this is what we're using to clean the place?"

"Florida Water makes the best floor wash. Unless you have bergamot oil, rose water, oil of neroli, and about seven other ingredients stashed in the van, we're going with this. Lots of cultures use tobacco to purify sacred spaces." She handed Jared a wet towel. "Start purifying."

Lukas walked up and down the stairs, refilling the bucket in the kitchen until Alara ran out of Red Cap and the floors were clean, at least according to her standards. He didn't say a word to Jared and not much more to me. When he caught me watching him, his usual playful expression was gone.

Alara lit a novena candle in the center of the room. By now, some of the children were sitting cross-legged around her, fascinated. "We need something to offer the loas."

I glanced at the stripped beds and the IV poles, the bare bulb and the dirty faces of the spirits. There was nothing here. Lukas and Jared looked through their pockets, but weapons and salt didn't seem like the right sort of offerings.

I only had one thing of value.

My hand shook as I slipped my mother's silver bracelet off my wrist and handed it to Alara. I heard a rip and turned in time to see Jared tearing something off his father's jacket. He dropped the white patch bearing his last name next to the candle.

Alara shook her head. "I'm not sure it's enough."

One of the smaller children scrambled to her feet and disappeared behind a metal bed frame. She scurried back and handed Alara a dirty bundle with two circles drawn on the front, and a piece of IV tubing wrapped around it. A crude doll made from one of the bed straps.

Alara's eyes glistened in the candlelight as she opened her journal and read from a page written in Haitian Creole, the language of the loas. The children listened intently and she turned to the next page, written in English—Psalm 136.

Her voice was quiet, and I only heard snippets as she spoke.

"To him who alone doeth great wonders:
for his mercy endureth for ever...
With a strong hand, and with a stretched out arm:
for his mercy endureth for ever...
And hath redeemed us from our enemies:
for his mercy endureth forever."

Their bodies started to fade, two or three at a time until there was nothing left but a patch, a silver bracelet, and a doll lying on the floor.

Upstairs, I lingered by the front door, trying to sense the change within the house. Part of me wanted to open the pantry in the kitchen to see if the spirit of the little girl was still locked inside. But I knew she was just a fingerprint left behind, and I wanted to remember the real spirits who had finally found a way out.

Jared was standing in the center of the rusty merry-go-round, staring past the gates over which no child would've been tall enough to see. From where I stood, the world was framed by those black bars. Had the children ever seen the world without them? Would they be able to see it now?

"When I was little, I wanted to be a superhero so I could protect people from the bad guys." Jared didn't look at me. "I couldn't even protect you from a dead kid."

"If you're talking about what happened today—"

"We could've died, Kennedy."

The front door slammed behind me.

"And whose fault is that?" Lukas stalked across the yard toward his brother.

"Do you really want to go there right now?" Jared stepped off the edge of the merry-go-round, sending it spinning without him.

"I want to know how many people are going to get hurt because of you. Are you gonna get her killed, too?" Lukas asked.

Time seemed to slow down as Lukas closed the distance between them. He lunged, tackling Jared, and they hit the ground hard. They rolled in the dirt, both grappling for the upper hand.

Jared made it to his feet first and grabbed Lukas around the waist, lifting him in the air. He slammed his brother's back into the dirt and pinned Lukas' arms down with his knees.

I ran down the steps just as Jared threw the first punch. "Stop it!"

Jared looked up at me. It was only a second, but it was enough time for Lukas to free one of his arms. His hand closed around Jared's throat.

"What happened in there wasn't Jared's fault or mine," I said. We all knew I was talking about more than getting trapped inside a wall.

Lukas relaxed his grip and Jared pushed himself away, coughing. "Don't worry, Luke. You made your point."

Lukas stood up and wiped the blood off his face with his sleeve before he walked away.

I knelt down next to Jared, and he dropped his head. "He's right."

"About what?"

"How close I came to getting us killed."

I didn't want to think about what it had felt like inside that wall. "We're both fine."

Jared looked at everything but me. "Because Lukas saved us."

"He had help."

"Lukas would've found you somehow. He protects people," Jared said, falling silent for a moment. "I get them killed."

"Don't do this to yourself. It was an accident."

He raised his head, eyes dark and shining.

"Five people are dead, and there was nothing accidental about it. I knew there was a risk, and I kept looking anyway. I led Andras right to them." Jared leaned his head against the wall. "I won't let you get caught in the cross fire the next time I screw up."

It felt like my heart stopped beating.

"What are you saying?" But even as I asked, I knew the answer.

He studied the weeds and dead grass at his feet. "I care about you—"

"Just not enough to stick around," I said.

Whenever I cared about someone, I imagined them leaving—the words they'd say, the way it would feel when they left. I thought if I prepared myself, it would be easier when it finally happened.

"You don't understand."

My hands curled into fists at my sides. "Three hours."

"What?" he asked.

"That's how long it took for you to walk away."

I was wrong.

"Kennedy—"

I held up a hand to silence him. "Now let's see how long it takes you to forget me."

29. SONS OF DISOBEDIENCE

I stared out the window as the winding back roads led us closer to the coordinates etched in the sledgehammer. I tried to lose myself in drawing, anything to forget Jared's arms around me inside the wall, or how easily he had given me up outside it. We hadn't spoken a word to each other since I left him standing in front of Hearts of Mercy.

There wasn't anything else to say.

Lukas had spent most of the ride searching websites on his cell phone, so he didn't have to talk to his brother. When he finally lost the signal, he went back to studying the map.

He drew a line connecting the red circles, while Jared scanned through the static on the radio.

"There's probably no reception out here." Priest looked

up from his own sketch, some kind of tube loaded with canisters.

"That's because this is the edge of the world, and we're about to fall off," Alara said.

Jared turned the dial again and this time a voice cut through the static. "The shooting occurred at eleven fifteen this morning at the Walmart in Moundsville. Three people were killed and two others injured before the gunman exited the store, turning his weapon on police."

"We must be getting close," Priest said.

"I found something else." Lukas held up the map. He had added blue Xs inside the boundary line.

Alara frowned. "You'll have to elaborate."

"The circles represent the places that had major surges in the last month, the cities and towns where we looked for Kennedy." He traced the line with his finger. "The Xs are the locations where we found pieces of the Shift."

Priest froze. "They're all inside that red line."

"So what does that mean?" Alara asked.

"I think the Marrow is in there, too," Lukas said. "And if I'm right, Andras is closer than we thought."

Alara nodded. "Then we need to find the last piece."

Another newscaster's voice replaced the first. "Eastern West Virginia is still under tornado watch. Two tornadoes touched down in Westover yesterday, destroying three homes and a community center. The National Weather Service is working to determine the cause—"

"It's like we're heading into it," Priest said.

Alara stared at the black clouds looming in the distance. "Or we're already there."

⊣ • ⊢

MOUNDSVILLE, WEST VIRGINIA

POPULATION 9,835

Jared glanced at the sign as we passed. "Only a few more miles." They were the first words he'd spoken since we left Hearts of Mercy.

The road curved and the sky turned black, but this time it had nothing to do with the clouds.

Alara leaned over the front seat to get a better look. "Please tell me I'm seeing things."

Hundreds of crows perched in the trees, crowded the telephone wires, and circled the sky.

Alara didn't take her eyes off the birds. "Black rain. That's what it's called when murders of crows gather in one place like this."

"Because they turn the sky black?" Priest asked.

"Because it's just as unnatural."

We moved closer to the birds churning purposefully over a spot in the distance. I didn't need to see the words etched in the sign we passed to know it was the West Virginia State Penitentiary.

The Gothic facade was flanked by high stone walls,

263

and the building looked more like a cathedral than a prison. Tangled razor wire littering the grass was the only clue that murderers, rather than holy men, once resided inside.

Lukas pointed at the arched entrance. "The coordinates are on the other side of that wall."

Alara shook her head. "I don't like this. My grandmother believed that crows could carry evil spirits to hell and back."

I looked up at the dark sky moving to the rhythm of thousands of black wings. "Then there were a lot of evil spirits in this place."

"Or they're still here."

We parked the van and stood in front of the concrete wall. ARE YOU BRAVE ENOUGH? was spray painted above a cracked hole that reminded me of the one in the basement of Hearts of Mercy. The names of people who had accepted the dare surrounded the opening. It was probably a rite of passage in a small town like this, something Elle would've convinced me to do with her before all this.

Now I was checking my pockets for paintball cases filled with holy water and kitchen spices, and a marker in case I needed to bind a spirit with a voodoo symbol.

Alara watched the crows, transfixed, as though she saw something more than their glossy black feathers and sharp eyes. "I have a bad feeling."

"Of course you do," Priest said, checking the pocket of

his hoodie for batteries and ammo. "We're about to break into a prison where hundreds of criminals died. This is the definition of a bad feeling."

"Are you saying we shouldn't go in?" she asked.

"I'm saying my granddad is dead because of Andras, and the Shift can stop him. I'm not leaving without it." Priest sounded older than when I first met him a few days ago.

Alara took one last look at the world on this side and followed Priest through the hole. "May the black dove always carry us."

Lukas glanced back at me before he climbed through, his eyes full of questions I knew he wouldn't ask. Questions that had been lurking around the edges of every look since the moment he broke through the boards at Hearts of Mercy and found me in his brother's arms.

I made a choice inside those walls, and there was no way to take it back. Because even if it was the wrong choice, how could I say that to Lukas when I had feelings for Jared?

"Kennedy?"

I didn't turn around.

Jared put his hand on the stones above my shoulder, his breath warm against the back of my neck. "I think we should talk before we go in there."

"We've talked enough." I slipped through the opening without looking back.

I couldn't afford to give him the chance to hurt me again.

Lukas waited on the other side with his hand out-stretched, offering to pull me up. I didn't look back at Jared when I heard him behind me.

The five of us walked across the cracked concrete basketball court, the only break in a sea of dead grass and twisted silver razor wire.

"Which way?" Priest asked.

"Northeast." Lukas pointed to the far corner of the building.

"Is there anything we should know before we go in?" I asked.

Other than the fact that we're walking into a haunted prison?

"Between the murders, suicides, and executions, hundreds of men died here. And Moundsville was the only prison in West Virginia with an electric chair."

"That's a serious body count." Priest examined the heavy double doors in front of us.

"That doesn't include the six people Darien Shears murdered," Lukas said.

"Who?" Jared watched the crows pecking one another on a broken picnic table.

"A couple of websites mentioned that Moundsville had its own serial killer."

Alara waved a hand in the air. "I've heard enough.

This is a paranormal minefield. Be careful where you step."

I never expected to see the inside of a prison.

The rows of thin rectangular windows didn't provide much in the way of light, for which I was secretly grateful. I didn't want a closer look at the dark stains on the concrete floors. Knowing people died here and seeing the evidence were two different things.

At the end of the narrow hallway, the metal door marked CELL BLOCK A stood wide open. Four floors of barred cell doors rose above and around us. Chain-link fencing covered the walls and the ceiling, creating one enormous cage. Trash, torn strips of bedsheets, and scraps of orange fabric littered the floor.

Something flickered at the end of the room—a blurry man in a jumpsuit the same fluorescent shade of orange. He was pushing a mop along the floor, when his head jerked up like he heard a sound from above. A second later, another hazy form fell backward over the top railing. The man with the mop screamed silently and tried to shield himself, crumpling beneath the weight of the falling man.

They both disappeared, and within seconds the man was pushing the mop again, the gruesome scene repeating itself in a never-ending loop.

I squeezed Priest's arm. "A residual haunting?"

"See, you're a pro now."

Even though I knew the men were nothing more than energy—handprints on a dirty window—the sight of the fall still made my pulse race.

Empty cigarette packs and burnt paper crunched under my boots as we followed Lukas to a door at the north end of the cell block. It opened into a hallway, part of the labyrinth of concrete tunnels burrowing through the guts of the prison.

Lukas found the northeast corner easily, a laundry room with industrial washers and dryers lining the back wall and a few wheeled laundry carts. More blood stained the floors beneath the rusted white machines.

Alara closed her eyes and ran her hand along the wall. "I don't think the Shift is in here."

Priest lifted an eyebrow. "Since when can you tell that from touching the wall?"

"It's just a feeling."

Lukas checked behind another washer. "I'd feel better if we checked the machines anyway."

Alara rolled her eyes and opened one of the dryers. She seemed more intuitive since the mark had appeared on her wrist, the same way Priest seemed braver after he earned his.

Did the marks change them, or did they change because of the marks? I wanted to ask, but the sting of envy stopped me.

"There's nothing here," Jared said. "We should go up to the second floor. I saw a stairwell at the end of the hall."

Priest jumped onto the first grated-metal step. "We're getting warmer."

"I'm not." My breath came out in white crystalline puffs.

The temperature continued to drop dramatically every few steps. When we reached the second floor, I understood why. The words *Death House* were spray painted in red on a windowless white door directly above the laundry room.

I rubbed my hands over my arms. "What do you think it means?"

"It's the room where they keep the electric chair," Priest answered. "In some prisons, electrocutions were held in a separate building. They called it the Death House."

"Look." Alara pointed at the gray metal door next to us. Words were written on this one, too:

Darien Shears

"That must have been his cell," Lukas said.

"Who?"

"The prison serial killer. A local war hero who was convicted of killing a girl who turned up dead after she left a bar with him. Shears swore he didn't do it, but the jury didn't believe his story and sentenced him to life. After a few weeks, prisoners started dying—stabbed in the shower,

269

strangled on the yard, suffocated in their sleep. Shears confessed to all the murders even though there were no witnesses."

Alara raised an eyebrow. "A serial killer with a conscience?"

"Who knows?" Lukas nodded at the white door. "But they executed him in the electric chair right there."

Shears' cell faced the Death House. If he looked out the tiny square window of his cell, the only thing Darien Shears could see was the room where he would take his last breath.

Jared peered through the square cut into the metal and froze. "No way."

"What?" Alara angled for a better look.

He unbolted the door, and the hinges groaned. The room was empty, but it didn't feel that way because every inch of the walls was covered with words, symbols, and pictures, overlapping in a dizzying pattern. In the center of the madness, one drawing stood untouched by the edges of the others.

The Shift.

It looked exactly like the one in Priest's journal, though clearly drawn by a different hand.

Priest pushed his way past Jared and stood in front of the enormous sketch. He reached out and held his hand over it, without touching the smooth concrete on which it was rendered. "It's not possible."

"Maybe Shears found the casing hidden in the prison," Lukas offered. The fifth and final piece of the Shift was the casing itself, the cylinder the four disks slid into.

Priest wasn't convinced. "But how did he know what the disks looked like? This sketch shows the Shift assembled."

As I scanned the walls, my mind memorized the pictures and symbols automatically. My eyes rested on the words scrawled over and over above the drawing of the Shift, words I knew I'd never forget: THE SPIRIT IS NOW AT WORK IN THE SONS OF DISOBEDIENCE.

Alara read them, too. "That's not crazy or anything."

"It's a verse from the Bible." Jared studied the wall. "But it should say, 'the spirit *that* is now at work in the sons of disobedience.' It's a reference to the devil. He's the spirit at work."

Demons were bad enough. I didn't want to deal with the sons of disobedience.

"There was something else in the article about Shears." Lukas hesitated. "When he confessed, he told the warden he was just a soldier following orders."

"You think the devil was giving him orders?" I couldn't hide the shock in my voice.

"I was thinking more along the lines of a demon," Lukas answered. "One that doesn't want us to find the Shift."

The hinges creaked again, and the heavy door slammed shut behind us.

A tall man stared wide-eyed like he had caught us

breaking and entering. His hair was buzzed down to nothing, pale eyes lost in the shadows of his gaunt face. A dark band of scarred skin cut across the man's forehead and circled his skull.

Every muscle in my body urged me to run, but there was nowhere to go. I couldn't tear my eyes away from him.

"I've been fighting this war too long to lose now." Darien Shears was still in the orange jumpsuit he was probably wearing when he died.

"There's no war." Lukas kept his voice even. "Nothing to lose."

We all knew it was a lie. The spirit stepped away from the door. It was covered with more writing: YOU DO NOT KNOW THE DAY WHEN YOUR MASTER IS COMING.

The spirit pointed at Lukas. "I sacrificed my life to protect it. Don't tell me there's nothing to lose."

It's still here.

My eyes darted around the room. There was nowhere to hide a cylinder the size of a coffee can.

Shears straightened. "I'm a good soldier. Stopped everyone who tried to take it. The same way I'm gonna stop you."

Priest raised the paintball gun. He fired off round after round, but the balls burst against the vengeance spirit's chest—holy water, salt, and cloves spraying onto the walls. I waited for the spirit to explode, but he only flickered for a second and vanished.

272

I stared at the paintball casings lying on the floor. "Why didn't they destroy him?"

"He's stronger than the average vengeance spirit." Lukas ran his hands along the walls checking for cracks. "The rounds weakened him, but I'm not sure how much. We need to find the last piece of the Shift before he comes back."

"It's not here," Jared said. "The walls are solid concrete."

"Then where is it?" I asked.

Alara stood in the doorway, staring at the view from Darien Shears' cell. "I think I know."

Alara kept her distance. "Do you think any of them were innocent?"

A crude wooden chair with heavy armrests was bolted onto a raised platform in the center of the room, like a dead man's throne. Padded leather wrist and ankle cuffs were buckled below the thick straps that secured the prisoner's chest to the chair. A coiled black wire snaked up the back and attached to a medieval-looking headpiece, with a metal band that matched the scarred skin around Darien Shears' head.

Lukas stopped in front of a row of numbered switches under the words CAUTION—HIGH VOLTAGE. "I don't know, but it looks like they all suffered."

Rows of hatch marks extended across the wall beside

the panel. Someone must've been keeping a tally of the men who had died here.

"Maybe they deserved to suffer." Jared sounded like the guy who burst into my house the first night I met him, not the boy I kissed inside the wall.

Echoes of murmuring voices bombarded us, too faint to decipher, and the unmistakable sound of frantic scratching coming from behind the walls.

"Well done, Jared." Alara sprinkled salt around the base of the chair. "Good to know you can piss off the living and the dead."

The scratching grew louder. Then all at once it stopped, plunging the room into an eerie silence.

Priest took a step back and bumped into the panel of switches.

"You're all monsters." A disembodied voice slithered through the room. "That's what they said right before they threw the switch."

Alara's body lurched back violently and she fell into the electric chair. The padded cuffs unbuckled themselves and closed around her wrists and ankles. The leather chest strap snaked around her torso and tightened, completely immobilizing her.

"Stop it!" she screamed.

Jared and Lukas struggled to unfasten the cuffs, but the leather straps held tight.

"Leave her alone, Darien," Priest shouted.

The voice laughed. "It's not Darien."

Faces appeared one by one, solidifying into full body apparitions—men still wearing their prison-issue orange jumpsuits. With their shaved heads and identical scars circling their foreheads where the metal had seared their skin, they looked like shells of the men who had died in the same chair where Alara was sitting now.

A man with dark shadows around his eyes stepped in front of her. "Do you have anything to say? They gotta ask you that before they throw the switch."

The one with empty gray eyes nodded. "It's the law."

"Let her go." Jared raised the semiautomatic paintball gun. "Or I'll give you a new set of burns."

Lukas aimed his own weapon and a vengeance spirit with a jagged scar across his cheek and the number thirteen tattooed on his neck smiled. "Ain't nothin' left to burn. Except your friend."

Jared and Lukas opened fire, the lethal mixture of holy water, salt, and cloves spraying across the walls until they ran out of ammunition. Two vengeance spirits exploded, but a half dozen stood fast.

Priest and I lifted our weapons.

Before I could squeeze the trigger, the gun was ripped from my hands.

I searched for a faded form, or the shadowy features of a spirit that wasn't fully materialized, but there was nothing.

Priest was disarmed the same way, his weapon floating in the air next to mine.

Our guns hovered for a moment, then turned and pointed directly at us.

Then the weapons changed direction, and the rounds discharged in rapid succession, hitting the tally marks on the wall over and over. When the ammo was spent, the weapons dropped at our feet.

"A prisoner built this chair. That seem right to you?" The spirit with the dark shadows around his eyes appeared. "Saying goes that if you die in this prison, your soul stays here. Don't matter if you're an inmate or not—no heaven or hell, just Moundsville." He lowered the metal cap onto Alara's head. "Let's see if your friend makes it out."

Alara screamed as Darien Shears materialized and clamped his hand over her mouth. He held a finger to his lips. "Shh."

Flashes of the prisoners' faces superimposed themselves over hers—the spirit with the shadows around his eyes, the one with the number thirteen on his neck—a parade of faces rotating in front of Alara's. Each man buckled and strapped in the chair, the metal headpiece secured to his skull.

Each one screaming and writhing in pain the way Alara was now.

Jared and Lukas ran for the chair.

"I wouldn't do that." Number Thirteen flipped the switches on the panel.

"It's okay," Priest said. "There's no power in this building anymore."

The vengeance spirit tilted his head, considering it. "Who said anything about using the building's power?"

The spirits focused on the control panel, and the indicators lit up one by one.

Oh god.

The last indicator blinked, but the light didn't fully illuminate.

"Shears," Number Thirteen called out. "We need more juice. Hit the generator downstairs."

Darien looked at Alara, then back at the rest of us. "Now don't go anywhere. Everybody will get a turn." He vanished, leaving the other vengeance spirits behind.

Priest reached under his hoodie and pulled out the caulking gun from the hardware store, the barrel loaded with purple cans of cheap hair spray.

What was he doing?

He aimed at the vengeance spirits and pulled the trigger, simultaneously igniting the fireplace starters wired to the end of the caulking gun. It was a makeshift flamethrower made from Aqua Net, electrical tape, and ingenuity.

A stream of flames shot out, and Priest scorched the

wall from left to right. The prisoners' faces contorted as the fire burned them to ash—and then nothing.

I knelt in front of the chair, unbuckling the stubborn leather cuffs.

"Come on!" Alara jerked against the restraints, her face streaked with tears. "Get me out of this thing!"

"I'm working on it." I fumbled with the ankle cuffs, pulling the last one free. Alara leapt from the chair.

My eyes were still level with the base. A single piece of wood attached the chair to the platform.

A piece shaped like a cylinder.

Someone had cut a crude notch in the wood. I held my breath and reached inside. The wood popped out, and a strip of silver glinted behind it.

My hand closed around the metal that felt as smooth and seamless as glass.

It looked exactly like the sketch in Priest's journal—strange looping symbols cut into the outside, and empty slots where the disks slid into place.

Lukas noticed the casing in my hand, his expression a mixture of awe and relief. "You found it."

Jared's eyes darted to the door. "We still have to get it out of here."

"Shears said he was coming back. He might catch us before we make it," Priest said. "We have to destroy him."

"How?" Alara's voice trembled.

The answer appeared in my mind slowly, like a print

developing in a darkroom. "I know what to do, but I need you to distract him."

Jared grabbed my arm. "What are you talking about?"

"I don't have time to explain." And I knew he would never agree if I did. "Do you trust me?"

The words hung between us—the question the four of them had been asking me all along. Now I was the one asking.

One by one they nodded and Jared spoke the words. "I trust you. But—"

"Then I need you to buy me some time."

Priest handed me the disks. "Take these just in case."

"No." I tried to push them back into his hand.

"Don't you trust me?" Priest gave me a lopsided grin, but his tone was serious.

I shoved them in my pocket.

"I'll buy you that time," Priest said before he turned to Alara. "You have to get back in the chair."

She stumbled away, her eyes wild. "Are you crazy? I'm not going anywhere near that thing."

Priest led her by the elbow as I took off down the hall. "It'll be fine. I'll disconnect the wires...."

I was the only person within these walls, living or dead, who wanted to get into a cell—especially the cell of a psychotic serial killer's ghost. But there was only one way to destroy him and if I was going to do it, I needed the element of surprise. And about eight minutes.

That was all the time it would take me to draw the one thing Darien couldn't use his disappearing act to escape.

The Devil's Trap.

I pictured the intricate design as I stepped back into Darien's cell—the pentagram inside the circle, within a heptagram inside another circle—every line, every shape, every letter of languages I didn't recognize.

The square cell was tiny. If I drew the outer circle big enough, the curved lines would touch the walls, leaving only the four corners of the room unmarked. Darien would have to step inside the symbol when he entered the room.

How can I get him in here?

It didn't matter unless I finished the Devil's Trap.

Shouts echoed from the other end of the hallway.

My hand started to move. I worked quickly, trusting the part of my mind that remembered the details on the face of a dollar bill, and the spot where every kid stood in our kindergarten class picture. I ignored everything else but the voice of my memory.

Seven names surrounded the circle—Samael, Raphael...

Looping the script perfectly, I copied the unfamiliar symbols like I'd written them hundreds of times. But I was careful, haunted by the entry in Jared's journal from the night the Legion summoned Andras.

What if I make a mistake?

I stopped, momentarily paralyzed by the thought, until a metal door slammed at the end of the hall.

My hand shook as I finished the last few details.

"Where are you?" an agitated voice called.

Darien.

How could I hide the Devil's Trap long enough to get him to step inside?

I glanced at the tiny window cut in the door, hoping

the spirit wasn't as close as he sounded. The opening was only about eight inches across. If I stood right in front of it, Darien wouldn't be able to see anything except my face. My knees buckled as I stumbled toward the door with the final piece of the Shift in my hand.

"I'm right here." I held up the cylinder, my face positioned in front of the window.

We were only a foot apart when his body passed through the door. I scrambled into the corner—one of the only places the curves of the Devil's Trap didn't touch.

Darien looked down, his feet firmly planted within the confines of the circle. His eyes mirrored the terror in the faces of the men that had flashed over Alara's in the electric chair.

He lunged forward until his fingers hit the edge of the circle. The supernatural force field threw him back into the center. "What have you done?"

"I think we both know." I huddled in the corner, clutching the Shift's casing against my chest.

"Kennedy!" Jared and Lukas called out, their footsteps getting closer.

Darien focused on the door. The metal rattled and the cell's heavy bolt clicked into place.

Bodies slammed against the door on the other side, and Lukas' face filled the small opening. "Are you okay?"

"Yeah." I slid my back up the wall until I was standing.

Drawing the circle up to the very edges of the walls had made it easier to trap Darien. Now I realized that it also made it impossible for me to get out.

"Don't move," Lukas said. "If you step inside the circle, he can hurt you. Stay there and the Devil's Trap should destroy him."

Should?

It sounded like something else they weren't sure about.

"How long will that take?" I asked.

"I don't know," Lukas answered.

What if he found a way to get out before then?

Darien ignored Lukas and pointed to the cylinder in my hands. "You have to put it back or innocent people will die. That's what she told me."

"Who?"

"The one who asked me to hide it."

"You mean the demon," Lukas shouted from the other side of the door.

Darien sank to his knees. His shoulders sagged as though he couldn't hold himself upright. The Devil's Trap was slowly killing him a second time. "A woman gave it to me. She told me I could redeem myself. Make my worthless life mean something."

What was he talking about?

"He's lying." I recognized Jared's voice immediately. "Vengeance spirits lie just like demons."

Darien frowned. "I killed six men in this prison protecting that thing and gave my life to the chair. That's no lie. You put that piece back where you found it before people get hurt outside these walls."

Jared's face appeared in the window. "Don't listen to him. He knows we can use the Shift to destroy Andras."

The spirit's eyes widened in horror. "The Shift doesn't destroy Andras. It frees him."

"What did you say?" I asked.

Darien spoke each word slowly. "If you assemble the Shift, it opens the gate."

"Liar!" Alara shouted from the hallway.

Panic spread through the spirit's hollow features, and he charged at me. I didn't have time to turn away before Darien hit the outer boundary of the circle again. His body convulsed like he was caught in an electrified fence. Then the force threw him back, and he slid across the concrete on his side.

"Kennedy, put it together now," Priest called out. "If the Shift can destroy Andras, it might be able to destroy him, too."

"I'll just wait until—"

Priest cut me off. "He's not giving up. What if he finds a weak spot in the circle?"

My hand shook as I searched my pocket for the disks.

I sat down and piled them in my lap. I slid the first disk

into the cylindrical casing. One of the symbols cut into the metal lit up, casting a beam of pure white light across the floor in the shape of the looping script.

Darien opened his eyes, still lying on his side. "I sacrificed my life to protect it for nothing."

"You didn't sacrifice your life," Jared snapped. "You were executed because you're a murderer."

My whole body trembled. "I should let you guys put it together. I can stay here until the Devil's Trap destroys him."

If it destroys him.

"Kennedy," Lukas pleaded. "You're too close to the circle. Don't give him the chance to break through and take it away from you."

I struggled with the next piece, sliding it into the wrong chamber before I realized each disk fit into a specific one. The second symbol emitted the same clean white light.

Darien crawled to the edge of the line separating us, so close I could reach out and touch him. "I killed men inside these walls. Evil men who tried to find the piece and give it to the servants of the demon. I promised to keep it safe."

Our eyes met, and I pressed myself flatter against the wall, trying to create distance where there was none.

My hands shook as I lined up the next piece, and I lost my grip.

The Shift rolled toward the edge of the Devil's Trap.

I scrambled for it, and Darien lunged at me again.

For a split second, it looked like his hands were going to cross the edge of the circle, or the cylinder was going to roll into the Devil's Trap. Darien hit the supernatural force field and my fingers caught the casing at almost the same moment—just as it reached the black line and Darien's body was hurled back into the center of the symbol.

"Kennedy!" Jared pounded on the metal door, but I didn't move. I couldn't.

I scooted back against the wall and slid the third disk into position.

Light poured from the arced shape.

Darien flickered, his cheek pressed against the cold floor I knew he couldn't feel. "I failed. We all did."

"Who?"

"Don't talk to him," Jared begged. "Just put it together."

"The spirits protecting the other pieces," Darien finished.

The last disk balanced between my fingers. All I had to do was slip it into place, but my hands weren't working. Every doubt about my mother's past, the Legion, and the four people who believed in me resurfaced.

What if I made the wrong choice?

"What if he's telling the truth?"

Jared pressed his forehead against the square opening. "Don't let him get in your head. You saw the journal. You know what it says."

Lukas shoved Jared out of the way, taking his place. "He's a vengeance spirit working for a demon. You can't trust him. Trust *us*."

Alara edged her way in front of the opening, her face blurred by my tears. "We're in this together."

"You're one of us," Priest called out from somewhere behind her.

I was tired of being afraid. I wanted to trust them—the people who meant so much to me now, the ones who believed in me.

"Kennedy, please." Jared took Alara's place, and his eyes found mine. This time he could see my tears. "We need you. I need you."

You can't choose the person who really sees you—the person who knows what you're feeling without you saying a word, the person who can make you laugh and cry and everything in between just by looking at you. The one you can't imagine being lucky enough to have, or unlucky enough to lose.

I was staring at him—the boy who was all those things and more.

My hand trembled as I aligned the final disk.

Darien faded, sputtering out like a candle burned to the wick. I snapped the disk into the casing and the final symbol illuminated.

Darien blinked one last time and whispered, "May the black dove always carry you."

I froze.

His spirit exploded.

The Shift grew hotter and hotter until it burned my hands. I barely felt it, paralyzed by Darien's last words.

May the black dove always carry you.

I dropped the cylinder, and a blinding light poured from the strange symbols as it rolled across the floor.

I thought about the other spirits—the girl in the yellow dress protecting her doll with the disk inside.

Millicent's words from the well: *"I won't let you take anything else from us."*

The magician's spirit promising he had tried to keep it safe before I destroyed him.

The disk hidden in a room protected by the spirits of dozens of dead children, and the words of the one carrying the sledgehammer it was hidden inside: *"If I watch over what's his, he'll come back for me."*

And Darien Shears, a serial killer who put the cylinder inside the base of the chair that electrocuted him—a spirit who knew the phrase used by the members of the Legion.

Were the spirits protecting the pieces all along, or did Andras' reach extend farther than we thought? Maybe Darien heard a member of the Legion say the words and remembered them?

I should have asked before I used my specialty to destroy him.

My specialty.

Salt spilled in between my fingers as I rubbed it over my wrist. I pictured the final section of the seal embedded in my skin and imagined my friends holding their arms against mine to complete the seal.

What will it feel like to be one of them?

I glanced at the Devil's Trap one last time to be sure. There was nothing inside, not a speck of dust. There was no doubt I had destroyed Darien's spirit.

But did I really trap a devil?

I waited for the lines to carve themselves into my wrist, hoping it wouldn't hurt. Familiar voices called out to me as I leaned over my arm, tears dripping down onto my perfectly smooth skin.

32. HEAT OF HELL

A crack snaked up the wall, destroying the perfect rendition of the Shift, as I watched the real one roll back and forth across the floor. I tried to pick it up and it burned the skin off my fingertips. The room shook, the low rumble of thunder trapped within the walls.

Maybe this evil place was coming down around me, and I'd never have to leave Darien's cell and face the four people who believed I was someone more than myself.

"Kennedy?" a voice called from the hallway.

I hugged my knees to my chest and waited to see if the building would stop shaking before I did.

Metal scraped and creaked as the bolt on the door unlocked.

Jared dragged me to my feet. "What are you doing? We have to get out of here."

I held out my arm silently, a thin layer of salt still coating my unmarked skin.

Confusion clouded Jared's beautiful features. Lukas and Alara came over as I rubbed more salt on my wrist.

Nothing.

Jared's face crumpled.

Lukas ran his fingers over the salt. "I don't understand. She drew the Devil's Trap. She destroyed Darien's spirit. We all saw it."

"My mark didn't show up right away. Give it some time," Alara said.

I fought to keep my voice steady. "Darien's spirit is gone."

Alara shook her head. "Something went wrong."

Not this time.

"Maybe—" Jared started.

"I'm not the one."

Jared's breath caught, and he closed his hand around mine. "There has to be another—"

I silenced him with a look. "There's only one explanation, and we all know what it is."

The floor buckled, and the ceiling split down the center.

Jared pulled my arm behind him, our fingers still intertwined. He looked down at me, our bodies practically touching. "It doesn't matter."

He was the boy inside the wall again—the boy who held me and confessed his deepest secret. The one I could trust.

"We both know it does."

Lukas reached for the Shift as it rolled across the floor.

"Don't touch it!" I shouted.

He pulled his hand back the moment his fingers grazed the metal. "What the hell?"

Alara wrapped her jacket around the cylinder and tried to pick it up that way, but the heat burned right through the fabric and she dropped it. "It's too hot."

"We have to go. Now." Jared shoved them toward the door, dragging me behind him.

Priest stood outside the cell, frozen. All the color had drained from his face. He grabbed Jared's arm and pushed the heavy metal door shut.

Pieces of concrete rained down on us, but no one moved. The letters that had spelled DARIEN SHEARS the first time we saw his cell door had rearranged themselves to spell something else:

anDraS is here

"Move!" Lukas yelled.

Lukas and Alara ran for the stairwell with Priest on their heels. The railing vibrated violently, and the shaking intensified as we navigated the stairs.

I slipped, and my knees slammed against the metal steps.

Jared hauled me to my feet, and we tore through the cell block. The deafening rattle of the bars rose up around us. Spirits flickered in our path, awakened by the sudden disturbance in their environment. But they weren't full body apparitions, and we passed right through them. Each time, I felt the revolting sensation of a cold hand tugging at the back of my neck, marking me in a different way.

Lukas burst through the door to the yard first. Instead of stepping into the afternoon light, there was nothing but darkness.

The black sky pulsed and churned like it was alive. Lightning cracked and illuminated thousands of beating wings, blocking out the sun.

Crows. Hundreds and hundreds of them.

Black rain, pouring from the clouds with no end in sight.

Alara stopped, fixated on the sky. She shouted something and took off in a dead run. I couldn't hear anything over the thunderous din of lightning flashing and feathers flapping.

It felt like the end of the world, the sky falling one dark wing at a time.

And it's my fault.

The van was only a few yards away now, the roof and windshield covered with more crows. They scattered when

Lukas opened the back doors, ascending to meet their own legion.

Priest tore open the duffel bags and unearthed the EMF detectors. He lined them up across the floor and flipped them on. The needles jerked all the way to the right, pushing into paranormal overdrive. Red bulbs flashed and the devices beeped, lighting up the floor like a pinball machine.

My heart pounded. "Does that mean there's something in here?"

"No." Priest stared through the window at the sea of black. "It's out there."

The EMF lights flashed faster and faster, blinking like the timer on a bomb.

"What's happening?"

Priest shook his head. "I don't know."

The EMFs exploded, wires and plastic ricocheting against the walls. I covered my head as sharp pieces of flying plastic sliced my arms, until the debris stopped banging against the van's interior.

A thin trail of blood ran down Alara's cheek. She winced, but instead of reaching for her face, she clamped her hand over the inside of her wrist.

Priest seemed confused for a second, then shook his own wrist, inhaling sharply. "My skin's burning."

Lukas nodded. "Mine, too."

Jared pulled up his sleeve. The mark that usually only

appeared when he rubbed it with salt was already carved into his skin. But the indentations weren't filled with dark lines. The mark was completely white, swollen red skin surrounding the outline. Lukas, Alara, and Priest revealed their marks one at a time.

I didn't have to check my skin to know it remained unmarked.

Alara shook her arm, trying to cool it. "What does it mean?"

We all knew, but no one wanted to say it.

So I did. "He was telling the truth."

Darien Shears. The spirit who tried to protect us from ourselves.

"No." Lukas rubbed his hands over his face. "The journal said—"

"Either the journal was wrong or we misinterpreted something." My voice faltered. "Look outside. Does it seem like I put together a weapon to protect the world, or used one against it?"

Real rain battered the roof, the sky still ink-stained from the clouds and the crows and whatever was coming next.

"It isn't your fault." Jared squeezed my hand. "We decided together."

I was the only one in that cell. I had snapped the pieces of the Shift together. It didn't matter if they had wanted me to do it or not.

In the end, I decided.

I had failed in too many ways to count, the proof destroying everything around us. Burning itself into everyone's flesh except mine—the one who didn't belong.

In a single moment, I had unleashed a demon their ancestors had spent over two hundred years defending the world against. One their families died trying to destroy.

33. BLACK DOVE

Sirens cut through the storm and the birds and the excruciating silence inside the van. Blue and red lights flashed through the darkness—police cars or ambulances, maybe both—and they were close.

"We have to run." Priest shoved everything within reach into one of the bags, and Alara did the same. With only one road in or out, we would meet those sirens head-on if we tried to leave the way we came.

Lukas opened the back door and rain pelted the metal floor. I couldn't see anything except the colored lights getting closer.

"If we get separated, head north." Jared pointed beyond the prison. "Pennsylvania isn't far. Find the second town closest to the state line, and we'll meet there."

Alara and Priest took off.

Lukas turned to follow them, and Jared grabbed his jacket. "Take Kennedy with you. She'll be safer."

Lukas and Jared faced their other halves, the person who made them both weaker and stronger. Neither of them spoke, but something more powerful than words passed between them.

Lukas shook his head. "You're faster."

Jared's eyes filled with doubt. "I don't want to screw up again."

"We all screw up." Lukas backed into the storm and disappeared in the darkness.

Jared's hand closed around mine, and we ran.

Our feet splashed through pools of water. Blood pounded in my ears and lightning cracked against the sky. I thought about the night my mom died—how scared I was and how alone. I was back in that place. In one moment, I had ruined any chance of destroying the demon that killed her, and I had endangered the lives of how many others? Thousands? Millions?

Jared swore the mark didn't matter, but I knew it did. And sooner or later, it would matter to the rest of them.

We reached the edge of the penitentiary, or what was left of the stone building. It looked like a child had built it out of blocks and knocked it over afterward. The sirens grew louder, the blue and red whirling lights practically on top of us.

We aren't going to make it.

"Come on." Jared led us deeper into the shadows. I tried to keep up, but the ground had turned into a river of mud, and I kept losing my footing. He tightened his grip on my hand as if he was determined not to let me fall.

The ground inclined, turning the gentle rise into an impossible climb as water and earth rushed under our feet. I lost my balance again. This time, my wet hand slipped out of Jared's and I fell.

My shoulder hit the ground, and I slid into something sharp.

Pain shot through my ankles and calves like hundreds of knives piercing my skin. I jerked and the feeling intensified. Was it glass?

Lightning splintered the sky, illuminating the silver vines coiled around my legs.

Razor wire.

I tried to pull my body free, but the wire only wound itself tighter, the barbs digging deeper into my flesh. I bit the inside of my cheek to keep from screaming, and the tang of blood filled my mouth.

Jared dropped down next to me, rain running down his face in rivulets. "Are you okay?"

I closed my eyes, trying to stay calm. "I think so" was all I could manage.

He smoothed the mud-slicked hair away from my face. "Don't move."

Jared tried to untangle the wire, but the metal teeth clung to my legs, and the nerves in my back seized. I winced and clutched his arm.

"Shh," he murmured. "I'm right here."

A car skidded through the mud, and a door slammed not far from us. We didn't have much time.

Lightning flashed again.

Jared's hands were soaked in blood from trying to unwind the silver ribbons curling around me. Prisons used this stuff for a reason. He wasn't going to be able to free me in the dark without wire cutters or an act of god.

I grabbed his collar and drew him closer, feeling the warmth of his breath on my face. "You have to go."

"I'm not leaving you." His voice cracked.

"Listen to me. People think I was kidnapped, and we just destroyed a prison. If you stay here, they'll arrest you."

"I don't care."

"I do." I held his face in my hands, forcing him to look at me even though we could barely see each other. "I won't be able to handle it if you get in trouble because of me."

You're already in trouble because of me. The whole world is.

Jared pressed his forehead against mine. The subtle shift in position sent another surge of pain shooting up my legs, and a wave of nausea rolled over me. He ran his fingers along the side of my face, and a different kind of pain consumed me.

"I shouldn't have pushed you away," he said.

All I could think about was protecting him. What happened between us outside Hearts of Mercy didn't change the way I felt about him. I wasn't sure anything could. "It doesn't matter—"

"Let me say this," he whispered. "I was scared. I still am. It's like you know me. You see things in me that no one else does." He shook his head. "I'm not saying this right."

I touched the scar above his eye. "You're saying it fine."

"I've never really had anything that was mine, and I never cared until now." He hesitated. "And I know you aren't mine...but I want you to be."

Boots splashed through the mud somewhere nearby.

I have to get him out of here.

I ran my fingers over his lips. "If Darien's spirit was telling the truth, I released a demon tonight. Think about all the innocent people Andras will hurt. You have to find a way to stop him, or I'll never be able to forgive myself."

It was a lie.

I would never forgive myself no matter what he did. But if Jared believed he was helping me, and the people caught in the trap I had unknowingly set, he might be willing to leave me here.

"Do you still care about me?" he asked.

I sensed him watching me. "We don't belong together. I'm not one of you."

His lips grazed mine. "Answer the question."

My breath hitched. "I care."

"It doesn't matter if you have a mark. You don't have to be anything more than you are." Jared pressed his lips against mine with a hunger that matched my own. For a moment, there was nothing but the two of us. He slid his mouth around to my ear. "You're enough."

"I'll check the west side," a voice called through the rain.

I ran my hand over his face, trying to memorize every curve and every line. "Please go."

"I'll find you, I swear," he whispered. "I—"

"Go." I shoved him away.

He hesitated, and I closed my eyes, listening as the storm swallowed the sound of his footsteps.

He's safe.

The pain subsided and numbness wrapped itself around me. I counted silently, praying he was far enough away, until the beam of a flashlight caught my eyes.

"Over here! I found someone." The officer bent down next to me. "You're gonna be all right, miss."

I didn't respond, hoping the rain would drown me. I searched for Jared's face in my mind.

Would I forget it? Or would my mind finally save a picture I wanted to remember?

I lay in the mud as the officers struggled to cut me free. "The ambulance is stuck in the storm, but we're gonna take good care of you. We've seen this kinda thing before. Haven't we?"

The other officer winced as the wire sliced into his hands. "We'll have you out of here in a few minutes, and your legs will be just fine."

What about the rest of me?

They asked my name over and over—when they bandaged my legs, when they wrapped me in a scratchy wool blanket, when I waited in the back of the police car. They would figure it out soon enough.

I was watching the rain pelt the ruined prison windows in the glare of the headlights, when something moved at the edge of the wall. Someone.

Jared.

Only a few yards away, but impossibly far in every way that mattered.

I'll find you.

I wasn't promising him. I was promising myself.

I had managed to lose everything all over again—the things I let myself want, and the ones I wanted so desperately to be true. But there was only one truth now.

I was never destined to save the world.

I was the one who destroyed it.

Even though I couldn't see more than his silhouette, I watched Jared until the officer climbed into the driver's seat and the tires spun through the mud. Until I couldn't see the prison or the road or anything except his face in my mind. I wondered if I would see it again.

And if the black doves would ever carry me.

ACKNOWLEDGMENTS

This is my Legion—the not-so-secret society of brilliant people who supported me throughout the process of writing this book and sending it out into the world. I am more grateful to them than they will ever know.

Jodi Reamer, the rock star of agents—for being the first and only agent to read this manuscript. I paced all night as you read it, knowing that if you loved the ending, you were the right person to take *Unbreakable* out into the world. Thank you for loving it and for answering a thousand e-mails and even more calls. You're in a class by yourself.

Julie Scheina, my first editor at Little, Brown—for taking this book all the way to the pass pages and pushing me to my limits in the best way. Working with you for the last six years was truly a gift.

Erin Stein, my editor at Little, Brown—for adopting me and *Unbreakable* as if we had been yours all along. Our shared love of *Buffy* and *Ghost Hunters*, and the fact that you knew Moundsville Prison is a real place, cannot be an accident. Your sharp eye, creativity, and belief in this book border on supernatural.

Team *Unbreakable* at Little, Brown—Hallie Patterson, for working publicity magic for me every day; Dave Caplan, for designing yet another cover to die (or kill) for; Pam Garfinkel, for giving me amazing editorial notes; Jill Dembowski, for helping me kill my darlings; Barbara Bakowski, for proving that copyediting is an art; Adrian Palacios, for the amazing trailer; Victoria Stapleton, for being a legend and the person who drives me to nail biting while I wait to hear if you love the book; Nellie Kurtzman, for being a marketing genius with supermodel hair; Melanie Chang, for being a PR guru; Andrew Smith, for being the smartest (and coolest) guy in publishing; and Megan Tingley, for believing in all my books from the start. I owe a debt to everyone at LBYR for your hard work. I am proud to call Little, Brown home.

Writers House, my literary agency—for inviting me to your party and representing me. Special thanks to Cecilia de la Campa, my foreign-rights agent, for shouting about *Unbreakable* from rooftops all over the world; and Alec Shane, for reading the book and loving it. I really do owe you a sword.

Kassie Evashevski, my film agent at UTA—for your talent, shrewd business sense, and genuine respect for authors and their books. There is no one better. Period.

My foreign publishers—for taking a chance on this book. *Merci. Grazie. Danke. Obrigado....*

Margaret Stohl, my friend and *Beautiful Creatures* coauthor—for making me write this book (and the others).

Melissa Marr, Kelley Armstrong, Carrie Ryan, Rachel Caine, Kimberly Derting, Margaret Stohl, and Cat Conrad—for listening to the first incarnation of *Unbreakable* and encouraging me to write it.

Holly Black and Carrie Ryan—for reading countless drafts and giving me round after round of revision notes. *Unbreakable* would be a different book without you.

Yvette Vasquez, Margaret Stohl, Melissa Marr, Rachel Caine, Tahereh Mafi, Richard Kadrey, James Scott Bell, Erin Gross, Shelby Howell, Jana Morgan, Nicole D'Amore—for reading and/or giving me notes. Most of all, for giving me courage.

Ransom Riggs, Rachel Caine, Ally Condie, Richelle Mead, and Nancy Holder—for writing amazing quotes that still make me blush.

Ghost Hunters Jason Hawes and Grant Wilson—for your quotes, which made every minute of research worth it. I am truly honored.

Chris Berens—for painting *Lady Day*, Kennedy's touchstone and the painting that inspired the title. Thank you for sending her to me.

Vania Stoyanova—for making me look great…and then making me straps.

Eric Harbert and Nick Montano, attorney and brand manager to the stars (and me)—for being two seriously stand-up (and badass) guys. I'm glad to have you in my corner.

Alan Weinberger—for making sure my knees hold up so I can go on tour.

Ekatarina Oloy—for taking my sketches and drawing a beautiful diagram of the Shift.

Del Howison (aka Dark Del)—for finding the Grand Pentacle when no one else could.

Viviane Hebel—for creating beautiful jewelry based on the book.

Michele Belanger—for knowing the facts about Anarel and sharing them with me.

Readers, librarians, teachers, booksellers, bloggers, and everyone who supported the Beautiful Creatures novels—for being the ultimate Legion and the reason I write. I hope you love *Unbreakable*. It's for you.

Mom, Dad, Celeste, John, Derek, Hannah, Alex, Hans, Sara, and Erin—for cheering me on in everything I do, no matter how crazy it seems. I'm the person I am because of you all.

Alex, Nick, and Stella—for believing I can do anything, even when I don't believe it myself. Without you, none of this matters. I love you.

CAGED

Iron bars were the only things separating us.

He sat on the cell floor, leaning against the wall, in nothing but a pair of jeans. I glanced at the chain binding his wrists. With his head bowed, he looked exactly the same.

But he's not.

I let my fingers curl around the wet bars. Several times a day, holy water rained down from the sprinklers in the ceiling. I fought the urge to unlock the door and let him out.

"Thanks for coming." He hadn't moved, but I knew he didn't need to see me to sense my presence. "No one else will."

"Everyone's trying to figure this out. They don't know what to do about—" The words caught in my throat.

"About me." He rose from the floor and walked toward me—and the bars separating us.

As he drew closer, I counted the links in the chain hanging between his wrists. Anything to keep from looking him in the eye. But instead of moving away, I gripped the bars tighter. He reached out and wrapped his hands around the metal above mine. Close but not touching.

"Don't!" I shouted.

Steam rose from the cold-iron bars as the holy water seared his scarred skin. He held on too long, intentionally letting his palms burn.

"You shouldn't be here," he whispered. "It's not safe."

Hot tears ran down my cheeks. Every decision we'd made up to this point felt wrong: the chains coiled around his wrists, the cell doused in holy water, the bars keeping him caged like an animal.

"I know you'd never hurt me."

The words had barely left my lips when Jared lunged at the bars. He grabbed at my throat and I jumped back, his cold fingers grazing my skin as I slipped out of reach.

"You're wrong about that, little dove." His voice was different, cruel and soulless.

Laughter echoed off the walls and chills rippled through me. I realized what everyone else had known all along.

The boy I knew was gone.

The one caged before me was a monster.

And I was the one who had to kill him.

Return to the haunting world of the *New York Times* bestselling Beautiful Creatures series with *Dangerous Creatures*, the first book in Kami Garcia and Margaret Stohl's brand-new series featuring fan favorites Link and Ridley!

Available May 2014
however books are sold

Ridley

There are only two kinds of Mortals in the backwater town of Gatlin, South Carolina—the stupid and the stuck. At least, that's what they say.

As if there are other kinds of Mortals anywhere else.

Please.

Luckily, there's only one kind of Siren, no matter where you go in this world or the Otherworld.

Stuck, no.

Stuck-*up*? Maybe.

Stupid?

It's all a matter of perspective. Here's mine: I've been called a lot of things, but what I really am is a survivor—and while there are more than a few stupid Sirens, there are zero stupid survivors.

Consider my record. I outlasted some of the Darkest Casters and creatures alive. I withstood whole *months* of Stonewall Jackson High School. Beyond that, I survived a thousand terrible love songs written by one Wesley Lincoln, a clueless Mortal boy who became an equally clueless quarter Incubus. And who, by the way, is not the most gifted musician.

For a while, I survived wanting to write him a love song of my own.

That was harder.

This Siren gig is meant to be a one-way street. Ask Odysseus and two thousand years' worth of dead sailors if you don't believe me.

We didn't choose for it to be that way. It's the hand we were dealt, and you won't hear me whining about it. I'm not my cousin Lena.

Let's get something straight: I'm *supposed* to be the bad guy. I will always disappoint you. Your parents will hate me. You should not root for me. I am not your role model.

I don't know why everyone seems to forget that. I never do.

No matter what Lena says, she was meant to be Light. I was meant to be Dark. Respect the teams, people. At least learn the rules.

My parents disowned me after the Dark Claimed me as a Siren on my Sixteenth Moon. Since then, nothing rattles me—nothing and no one.

I always knew my incarceration in the sanitarium that my Uncle Macon called Ravenwood Manor was a temporary pit stop on the way to bigger and better, my two favorite words. Actually, that's a lie.

My two favorite words are my name, Ridley Duchannes. Why wouldn't they be?

Sure, Lena gets the credit for being the most powerful Caster of all time. Whatever. It doesn't make *me* any less excellent. Neither does her too-good-to-be-true Mortal boyfriend, Ethan "the Wayward" Wate, who defeats Darkness in the name of true love every day of the week.

So what?

I was never going for perfect. I think that should be clear by now.

I've done my part, played my hand, even thrown in my cards when I had to. I've bet what I didn't have and bluffed until I had it. Link once said, *Ridley Duchannes is always playing a game.* I never told him, but he was right.

What's so bad about that? I always knew I'd rather play than watch from the sidelines.

Except once.

There was one game I regretted. At least, one that I regretted losing. And one Dark Caster I regretted losing to.

Lennox Gates.

Two markers. That's all I owed him, and it was enough to change everything. But I'm getting ahead of myself.

It all started long before that. There were blood debts to be paid—though this time it wasn't up to my cousin and her boyfriend to pay them.

Ethan and Lena? Liv and John? Macon and Marian? This wasn't about them anymore.

This was about Link and me.

I should've known we wouldn't get off easy. No Caster goes down without a fight, even when you think the fight is over. No Caster lets you ride off into the sunset on some lame white unicorn or in your boyfriend's beat-up excuse for a car.

What's a Caster fairy-tale ending?

I don't know, because Casters don't get to have fairy tales—especially not Dark Casters. Forget the sunset. The whole castle burns to the ground, taking Prince Charming down with it. Then the Seven Dwarfs go all ninja and drop-kick your butt straight out of the kingdom.

That's what a Dark Caster fairy tale looks like.

What can I say? Payback's a bitch.

But here's the thing:

So am I.

KAMI GARCIA is the #1 *New York Times* bestselling coauthor of *Beautiful Creatures*, which is now a major motion picture. *Unbreakable* is her first solo novel and the first book in the Legion series. Kami lives in Maryland with her family and her dogs, Spike and Oz, named after characters from *Buffy the Vampire Slayer*. You can find her online at kamigarcia.com and on Twitter @kamigarcia.